GROWING SEASON

GROWING
SEASON

•

MIKE GAHERTY

AVALON BOOKS
THOMAS BOUREGY AND COMPANY, INC.
401 LAFAYETTE STREET
NEW YORK, NEW YORK 10003

PRINTED IN THE UNITED STATES OF AMERICA
ON ACID-FREE PAPER
BY HADDON CRAFTSMEN, BLOOMSBURG, PENNSYLVANIA

To my wife, for her inspiration, patience, and advice—
with love

Chapter One

Katie Rourke's eyes left the road long enough to focus on the lights of Willow Grove, still five miles in the distance. She was tired. She had left Rockford, Illinois, nearly five hours ago. She saw the three red lights of the antenna for KPTI, ''the radio voice of Iowa's heartland.'' To the right but not as high was the steady red light that she knew marked the top of the town's water tower, a light blue affair with WILLOW GROVE lettered boldly around its side. When she was little, it had always reminded her of an upturned bicycle horn. The kind with a rubber bulb you squeeze to blow it. But it was too dark to see its shape tonight. She knew she could pick out her town from the scores of little towns she had passed in the last five hours. She could do it day or night, it made no difference. And she could do it with just a glance, her brain having long ago memorized the shapes and lights that marked it.

Why should I still call it my town, she thought. Rockford, Illinois, was her home now. Why, she hadn't used Willow Grove as a mailing address since going off to college more than eight years ago. But still, when friends at the high school where she taught or at the apartment complex where she lived asked what she was doing over spring break or Christmas vacation, her answer, often as not, was, ''I'm heading home for a few days.'' Her eyes filled with tears at the thought and the distant lights blurred. She reached for a tissue. *It won't seem much like home now, without*

Mom and Dad, she thought. She slowed and nudged the turn signal for a right turn. A tree, a giant cottonwood, marked the gravel road leading to the farm. She could just make out its dark shape as she reached the intersection.

Katie made the turn and adjusted her speed to the loose gravel surface. She could hear the familiar sound of the rocks spraying up from the wheels against the underside of the car. As she reached the top of the hill and caught sight of the familiar lights of the comfortable farmhouse, the nightmare that was now little more than a month old came rushing back as she knew it would. The look in the principal's eyes as he called her out of her classroom. The feeling of total hollowness as she hung up the phone in his office. The long trip back home, alone, with only her thoughts to torment her. And the eyes of her grandmother— those eyes of loss and sadness. ''I should have been with them,'' Gram had said over and over, as if she were somehow to blame for the accident.

As she reached the driveway, Katie felt the return of guilt for having left her grandmother alone, if only for a week. She had taken her full bereavement leave and then Christmas break followed. But she had to get back to school to finish final grades and arrange for a semester's leave of absence. It wasn't that she hadn't tried to take her grandmother back to Illinois with her. After all, there was plenty of room in the apartment. But Gram absolutely refused, and Katie knew that look. She had agreed to leave only after neighbors promised to keep a close watch on the little lady. Katie grimaced at the thought of the battle she had on her hands to try to convince Gram to move to Illinois before the start of the next school year, after the land had been rented and the affairs settled. She set her jaw. *There's no way I'm going to leave a seventy-five-year-old woman out on a farm by herself, no matter how feisty she is.*

She slowed for the driveway and made the familiar turn on to the rock-covered lane. The light mounted near the peak of the garage was on, throwing a circle of white over the front porch and the snow-crusted lawn and a dark blue pickup parked in the drive. She pulled to a stop next to it. The neighbors are true to their word, she thought to herself with a sense of relief. Sugar, the black and white springer spaniel, a member of the family for over ten years now, bounded down the front steps. She blocked the path to the porch and barked excitedly. Katie opened the car door. "Hey, what's the matter, girl? It's just me."

The old dog heard the familiar voice and ran to the car, placing her two front paws on the bottom of the door frame, blocking Katie's way. Katie cradled the dog's head in her two hands. "Glad to see me, girl? Yeah. You're a good girl, aren't you?"

She slipped her legs carefully past the dog and stepped out of the car just as the front door opened and her grandmother stuck her head out. Katie took a deep breath to prepare herself for what would forever be a changed homecoming, pulled one of her suitcases out of the backseat, and lugged it toward the door. She set it down to hug her grandmother, who had stepped out onto the porch. "Gram, you're shaking. Is anything wrong?" She held the frail shoulders and looked into her grandmother's clear, pale blue eyes.

"No, dear, everything's just fine now," she answered. "I just thought you'd be here earlier, and now it's almost seven-thirty."

Katie felt guilty all over again. She must be remembering that horrible day too. And Katie could have called just as well as not, so Gram could have known when to expect her. "I'm sorry. I got on the road later than I thought, and there was a big slowdown near Dubuque."

Grandma patted Katie's hand. "That's all right. I know I've got to get over this silly worrying. And I will, too. Anyway, I had that nice David Cairn from up the road to keep me company." She slipped her arm around Katie's waist and walked her toward the front door. "We'll get your things later. You remember David, don't you, dear? I bet you two were in school together."

"I wondered whose truck that was," Katie said, as she tried to keep pace with her grandmother, all the while dragging the big suitcase by her side. She smiled to herself. David Cairn? Oh, yes, she remembered him all right. Little did her grandmother know. In fact, she thought, little did anyone know, especially David Cairn himself. The love of her life when she was thirteen, and he was a senior in high school. Come to think of it, the love of her life from the time she first figured out there was a big difference between girls and boys. Then he graduated from high school and went on to college in Ames and was lost to her forever. Years of fantasizing down the drain. She followed her grandmother down the hall toward the brightly lighted kitchen. And there he was, David Cairn himself, sipping coffee at the kitchen table.

As she entered behind her grandmother, he got to his feet, scraping the legs of the padded vinyl chair on the linoleum floor. She checked him out. He was a pleasantly filled-out version of the boy from her past. She hadn't seen him for years, but she instantly remembered those dark brown eyes, eyes that liked to settle on what they focused on until they were satisfied. But right now those eyes seemed more inquisitive than anything. He still had that unruly shock of hair that hung down over his forehead, and she was glad to see he hadn't given in to some gel or oil to try to tame it. His hair was darker now, but maybe that was because she remembered it bleached by the summer sun. He had just the beginning of furrow lines on his forehead, just above the bridge of his nose, but they had the effect of making him appear, if not wise, at least thoughtful. He seemed taller than she remembered, but probably because she was seeing him in a room, not in a field or on a gymnasium floor. He cleared his throat and moved his chair with his legs with a touch of nervousness, as if he had something that had to be taken care of.

"Hey, Squirt, you sure have grown up."

So he did remember her, she thought. And naturally he'd remember that horrible pet name.

He smiled, and it was that same delicious smile of old. "I don't suppose you care much to be called that anymore?"

She smiled back with a look that answered his question. *He must not know he's the only one who ever called me that,* she thought. She reached her hand across the table to him. "Hi. It's good to see you again after all these years. Thanks for keeping an eye on Gram."

He reached for her hand eagerly, as if it reminded him of what he wanted to say. He held it in one large hand and covered it with the other. "I'm sorry about your mom and dad. I talked to your dad just before we left for Arizona." His words came faster then. "I took the folks down there for Christmas at my sister Beth's place, where they're spending the winter. Wanda Elmon called us about the accident. Mom wanted to come right back for the funerals, but there's no way you can get Dad on a plane, and there wasn't time to drive. I just got back last week, the day after you left." He became aware he was still holding her hand across the table and released it suddenly. "We're going to miss your folks around here, that's for sure. The neighborhood and everyone in town is still in shock. I'm just sorry I wasn't here to help out."

Katie blinked back a tear and took a deep breath, and let it out in a sigh. "Thanks. Everyone around here has been unbelievable. At times like this, you really know what it means to have friends."

He fingered the top of the table. "So your grandma here tells me you're living in Illinois now. Rockford, she says."

Katie glanced at her grandmother, who was standing by

the stove smiling as she watched the two. "Right. I teach English at Herreman High School."

"I had a friend in college from Rockford. Maybe you know him. Mark Saunders? That was a few years ago. He was in vet school, and I'm pretty sure he went back home to set up a small-animal clinic."

Katie shook her head slowly. "No, can't say I've ever heard of him. But it's a pretty big place. And I don't have a dog or cat. Not that I wouldn't like to, but they're not allowed in our apartment building." She knew she was rambling, and she looked toward her grandmother for help, but got nothing but another smile for her trouble.

"Uh-huh. Well, it would be quite a coincidence if you knew him." He reached for his coffee cup to give his hands something to do, and studied her face in the process. Was this really the same gawky kid who used to hang around all the time? He admired the fine features of her face, her perfect complexion, and the delicate mouth that seemed to smile so easily. *And that red hair is spectacular,* he thought. *I like it like that, to the shoulders and flipped up. Does she really have eyes like that? No one has eyes like that. Maybe she has contacts, but I don't think so. What would you call that? Aquamarine?* He took a step away from the table and reached for his coat, which was draped over the back of the chair. *Nothing wrong with the rest of her either,* he noted. "Well, I'd better get going. You probably want to eat and get settled in. Can I help unload your car or anything?"

"No, no, that's fine. I already brought in the heaviest suitcase. I've just got a few odds and ends left." She moved out of his way as he started for the front door. He towered over her as he passed, and she had to crane her neck to look up into his face. "Thanks again for keeping an eye on Gram."

He stopped and smiled over her head back at Grandma Pitcher still standing by the stove. "I assure you it was my pleasure. Anyway, the big question is, who was keeping an eye on whom? Right, Mrs. Pitcher?'' He laughed, and the sound was definitely welcome in this house, where it had been missing for more than a month now. ''Anyway, I wasn't alone. There was a whole flock of neighbors checking in, wasn't there, Mrs. P? You must have been worn out making coffee.''

Katie followed him out the door to get the rest of her things from the car. As she pulled a clothes bag from the backseat hanger, she stopped to watch his pickup pull out of the lane onto the gravel road. *Did I hear him right?* ''Who was keeping an eye on whom?'' She shook her head. *I admit it. We English teachers are a royal pain. No wonder people are afraid to open their mouths around us. They think we're picking apart their grammar. But not me. No, I'm surprised when someone gets it right.* She threw the garment bag over her arm and reached for a smaller suitcase. *So big deal; he's a literate farmer. There are lots of literate farmers. Dad used to read Shakespeare.* She watched the taillights of his truck fade up the road before she turned for the house. She found herself even more intrigued with this David Cairn now than she had been thirteen years ago.

Katie set down her suitcase, threw open the front screen door, grabbed the bag again, and tried to hop in before the swinging door caught her. She made it, but the door smacked loudly against the end of her suitcase.

''Do you need some help there?'' Gram shouted from the kitchen.

Katie stumbled into the kitchen with her load. ''No, I'm okay. I've got some things in the trunk, but they can wait till tomorrow.'' She stepped into the living room and spread the clothes bag on the sofa. Then she returned to the kitchen and fell into a chair. ''I'm exhausted.''

''I'll bet you are. And you must be hungry. I'm heating up supper. I fixed enough for both of us, because I didn't know what time you'd get here. There's meat loaf and green beans and scalloped potatoes and apple pie for dessert. How does that sound?''

"Great. You must have been slaving away in the kitchen all afternoon."

"Oh, you!" Gram said with a smile. She slid a plate and silverware in front of her granddaughter and began to set the casserole dishes of steaming food on the gray Formica table. She stopped when she saw the pie. "What in the world is going wrong with my brain? I should have offered David a piece of pie. I had it sitting right on the counter, and I bet he saw it too. What must he think of me?''

Katie had already started to load her plate. "I imagine he thinks you're pretty special. How could he think anything else? Anyway, I saw that smile he gave you when he was leaving." She looked innocently across the table at her grandmother, who had pulled out a chair to sit down. "Is there something going on between you two?''

Grandma clicked her tongue against her teeth and feigned a shocked look, but such teasing had always been a way of life between the two. She jutted out her chin. "I'll tell you one thing, young lady, if I were forty years younger, I wouldn't let that fellow get away."

Katie grinned at her grandmother between bites of scalloped potatoes. "Come on, Gram, this is the '90s. Go for it. Liz Taylor did."

"And look what happened with those two." Her voice took on a serious tone. "He's such a nice young man. He needs a woman who appreciates him. Not like that flibbertigibbet that he was married to. That woman must have oatmeal where her brains ought to be." Gram was warming to the subject, and she had Katie's undivided attention.

"So what happened with them?"

Grandma shook her head in disgust. "I know it takes two to break up a marriage, but not in this case. No sir. It was all that woman's fault, believe you me. They met in college. She was in law school. From Denver. Now whatever brought her all the way from Denver to go to school in Ames, Iowa? Don't they have schools out there?''

Katie suppressed a laugh. "Sure they do, but Iowa State is a good school. Maybe she had family around there or something.''

"I don't think so. Well, anyway, she thought she was some kind of big-time lawyer. John Lancome took her into his office here in town, but that wasn't good enough for Miss High and Mighty. No, she didn't like the kind of cases she got to work with. So guess what she did? She took a job in Des Moines with some big firm. In Des Moines! Can you imagine? More than two hours away. She came home on weekends. Big of her, I'd say. If that won't ruin a marriage, nothing will.''

Katie was making serious headway on the plateful of food in front of her, but now she stopped to stare across the table at her grandmother. "How in the world do you know all this?''

Grandma raised her head with a knowing look. "Oh, I keep my ears open. You pick up a little here and a little there.''

"Sure. Have you ever thought of CIA work? I bet they could use your talents.''

"Well, make fun if you want to, but I still say David Cairn deserves better than he got.''

You won't get an argument from me, Katie thought to herself. She pointed to the pie. "Since you cheated that fine young man out of his pie, that must mean I get an extra big piece. Right?''

Katie had put her clothes away upstairs, and now she sat in the spacious living room, in her mother's favorite recliner, a mug of coffee nestled in her hands. Her grandmother was working on her latest counted cross-stitch by the light of a bright gooseneck lamp.

"What are you working on now?" Katie asked.

Her grandmother held up the package so Katie could see the design, a robin sitting on a nest with the message, THERE'S NO PLACE LIKE HOME.

Katie smiled. "That's cute. How many of those things have you done anyway? About a thousand?"

"Well, not that many, but quite a few. It gives me something to do in the evening." She looked off into space. "Nowadays, it helps take my mind off things."

Katie nodded. "I know what you mean. I worked my brains out this past week to try to forget." She took a sip of coffee. "Maybe when you go back to Rockford with me in the fall, we can find some volunteer work you can sink your teeth into."

Grandma looked up quickly from her work. "We're not going into that again, are we? I told you I'm not leaving here. I can take a little apartment in town. I've got my friends here and my bridge clubs."

Katie took a deep breath. Maybe this wasn't the time to push, but she meant to chip away at her grandmother's stubbornness. "Well, at least think about it, would you, Gram? I'd feel so much better having you close."

Grandma Pitcher jabbed the needle through the material stretched on the round wooden frame. "I already have thought about it, and my mind's made up."

Katie set her coffee cup on the end table by the side of the chair. The subject was still a tender one, Katie could see, but she had seven months, time to do lots of convincing. She knew she had her work cut out for her, though. She remembered the struggle her folks had in the first place just three years ago getting Grandma Pitcher to give up an apartment in town to come live with them. "Don't get all worked up," she said. "We can talk about it later." She stretched and yawned noisily. "I'm going to head up to bed. It's been a long day. I've got to call Mr. Peters early tomorrow and see if I can make an appointment to start going over the folks' stuff. The bank promised he'd be back this week.''

Gram set her needlework in her lap and looked across at Katie. She took off her wire-rimmed glasses and dabbed at the corners of her eyes. ''I'm sorry, dear. I shouldn't have barked at you like that. I don't know what's gotten into me. You know what I think of you, and there isn't anything that could change that.''

Katie stood and put her hand on her grandmother's shoulder. ''And I feel exactly the same about you. The two of us have got to stick together now to get through all of this.'' She patted her grandmother's arm. ''I'll see you in the morning. Good night.'' She trudged slowly up the stairs to her room. She knew she needed a good night's sleep to prepare her for tomorrow's ordeal.

Chapter Two

Stanley Peters stood by the large window behind his desk at the Willow Grove Farmers' State Bank. He was a man of fifty-five who had been with the town's only bank for thirty-two years, working his way from the teller cage to his own private office where he counseled local farmers and the people of this tiny town about some of the largest money transactions many of them would ever make in their lifetimes. He was a short, stocky man who would never appear on the job in anything other than a dark suit with a white shirt and tie. He had a perpetually flushed face, and his head was quite bald except for long, gray hair he combed over from one fringe to the other. He was a pleasant enough fellow, with a ready smile. Today he stood with his hands clasped behind his back watching through the wide wooden venetian blinds as Katie Rourke stepped out of her car, parked on the corner by the town square, and fished through her purse for spare change to plug the parking meter.

He smiled. He was remembering the very first time she had come to the bank with her father. She must have been three years old, he guessed. She started to whimper as the solid, ornate door closed behind the two. And then the whimper grew to a healthy cry and the healthy cry became a wail until a red-faced Tim Rourke carried the little girl back outside into the bright sun. Stanley remembered that the two didn't return that day, and, in fact, Katie didn't come calling for another two or three years at least. Tim confided later that the cages surrounding each of the teller windows had frightened her. That was before the interior of the bank had been modernized. In the workings of her mind, she became convinced she was about to be locked up in some jail.

He watched her cross the street, thinking to himself what a striking young lady she had become, with her blazing red hair and delicate features. She could pass for one of those big-time models, he decided, except she's got more meat on her bones. He walked around his desk toward the door to meet her, not looking forward to the delicate chore ahead of him. He knew what he had to tell her would not be welcome news.

He held out his hand. "Katie, it's so good to see you." His face clouded. "But not under these circumstances, of course."

"I know, Mr. Peters." She followed him into his office and took the chair he offered her in front of his spacious, cluttered desk. "I really appreciate your seeing me on such short notice."

He waved his hand. "What do you think this is? The Chicago Mercantile?" he asked with a twinkle in his eye. "Around here, we're just glad to have someone drop by to take the boredom out of our day." He slipped behind his desk and into the waiting swivel chair. Leaning forward, he wrapped the stubby fingers of one hand nervously around a crystal paperweight and put on a somber face. "I'm still in shock about your folks, Katie. We left right after the funerals for Florida and just got back last week. I'll tell you one thing, it makes a person think. Both your mom and dad were younger than me. You just never know what's going to happen when you crawl out of bed in the morning. And to lose both of them at the same time. . . ." He shook his head. "It must be just about more than you can handle."

"It hasn't been easy, that's for sure. Thank God I still have my grandmother. We've both been holding each other up."

Mr. Peters smiled and leaned back in his chair. "Ah, yes, Esther Pitcher. What a good soul." He swiveled slowly from side to side and watched Katie's blue-green eyes. "Tell me, how is she getting on? Seems to me she wasn't in the best of shape when she moved in with your folks. What's that been, three, four years?"

"Three years. She'd just had surgery and Grandpa had died about four or five months before that, so she was kind of shaky for a while. But in the last year or so she's really come around. In fact, Mom was worried because Gram had been making noise about moving back to town into an apartment of her own. Mom didn't think she was strong enough for that. Now I'm afraid I've got the same problem. I was hoping to take her back to Rockford with me, but it seems she has other ideas."

"Uh-huh." He slid a tan folder to the center of his desk and drummed on it with the fingers of one hand. "I've noticed that old folks get kind of set in their ways." He glanced up and flashed the grin that Katie remembered from her earliest days at the bank. "Course, I don't suppose we'll be like that when we get to their age. We'll be just as sane and reasonable as we've always been. Right?"

Katie smiled her agreement. "I suppose we'll think we are anyway."

"Just like they think they are, I guess," he added. He opened the folder and pulled out several documents. "I know you've been through the lawyer stuff with the will and all, and now I guess it's up to me to bring you up to speed on the money matters. I think we handled all your folks' affairs here at the bank, isn't that right?"

Katie nodded. "As far as I know. Dad and Mom have been coming here for as long as I can remember."

Mr. Peters had perched a pair of dark-rimmed half

glasses on the end of his nose, and now he peered over them at her. "Tell me, Katie, what are your plans with the farm?"

She shifted uneasily in the chair. Mr. Peters always got right to the point. No beating around the bush, her dad would say. And that's why he never wanted to do business with anyone else at the bank. "Well, I've been running this over and over in my head," she began. "What I thought I'd do is rent out the land on the shares or for cash rent, whichever works best. Then I'll use the rent money to pay off what's left on the hundred and sixty acres the folks bought a few years ago. I know Dad has a lot of good machinery, so I was hoping we could have an auction to sell that off. And I was hoping to rent the house to a good family." She sighed. "Then I'll see if I have any luck moving Gram back to Illinois with me. I took a leave of absence for this semester, so they're expecting me back in September." She shrugged her shoulders. "That's about it, I guess."

Now it was the banker's turn to twist uncomfortably in his chair. The man who was never at a loss for words was strangely quiet. "Uh-huh. Well," he began slowly, "I'm afraid what I have to tell you isn't going to make you happy, and I'm sincerely sorry for that."

Katie sat up straight in her chair. "What do you mean?"

"You'll want to run the numbers yourself, of course, but I don't see any way you can generate the money you need by renting."

Katie was shocked at what she heard. Her face registered her confusion. "I don't understand. Dad had two hundred and forty acres completely paid for. I know that. He bought another hundred and sixty just . . ." She scratched her forehead. ". . . about eight years ago, wasn't it?" Mr. Peters nodded. "I know I can get a hundred dollars an acre in a straight cash rent deal. Right?" Again, he nodded. "That's forty thousand dollars. I know, I know, I'm not figuring in taxes and probably some other things, but still, they can't be that much. There's got to be enough left over for the payments on that new land." She added quickly, "I don't need any of the money myself, you understand. I've got my own job. I just want to plow it back into the farm for now, at least till I get the new place paid for."

Mr. Peters shuffled through several papers in the folder before he looked up at her again. This time he took off the glasses, which he knew made him look too official. "How well do you know your folks' financial affairs?"

She met his gaze. "Not very well, I guess."

"Uh-huh. Well, I'm afraid things took quite a tumble for them here of late." He hurried on, aware of her shocked look. "Your dad was forced to sell his fat cattle just before Thanksgiving. He lost a bundle, but knowing him, I'll bet he never let on to you." Katie felt the tears well in her eyes. Mr. Peters was right. She had spent Thanksgiving at home, but she never suspected and not a word was mentioned about any trouble. "In fact, I'm not really sure your mother knew how bad it was. He kept the cattle longer than he should have, but he was waiting for an upturn in prices which never came. He had five hundred head. Did you know that?" Katie shook her head. There was a shocked look in her eyes. "He bought too high, and he bought too many. He wanted to make one big killing. He wasn't alone, you understand. A lot of farmers around here were doing it. I think he wanted to make enough so he and your mother could take it a little easier. It's all water over the dam now, but believe me when I tell you, I did try to talk him out of it—at least out of buying such a big herd of feeder cattle. It's always risky to assume the price is going to hold steady, or even go up. And I told him that."

The room was spinning for Katie. She didn't say anything for a time. When she finally did speak, her voice was barely audible. "How bad is it? We're not going to lose the farm, are we?"

"No, no, no, it's not as bad as all that. You're going to come out of all this in decent shape. It's just that I don't think you can hold on to all the land."

"But what about the machinery? Wouldn't an auction bring in enough to cover the loss?"

"I'm sorry to tell you that's more bad news." He pulled more documents from the folder. "Your dad bought a new tractor two years ago and a new combine just last year."

She knew about both of those, and remembered being stunned when she found out how much they had cost. You could buy a really nice house for what those two pieces of machinery had cost. Her dad had let her pick one round of corn with that mammoth machine all by herself when she was home last fall. "He was so proud of that darned combine," she said softly.

Stanley Peters wondered why he could never feel such pride of ownership in anything. To him, a car was meant to get you from one place to another. And a car five or six years old that had long ago lost its showroom smell could do the job just as well and for a lot less money than a brand-new shiny one. He hated himself at times for seeing things with such a banker's mentality, and today was definitely one of those times. He said flatly, "I never saw it, but I knew he was proud of it. The trouble is, he still owes nearly a hundred thousand dollars on it and the tractor. I tried to talk him into taking out the standard life insurance package to cover those two loans, but he was never big on insurance. He always said that the farm was his insurance, which is true in a sense. But then, like most of us, he was expecting to live to be a hundred."

Katie leaned forward in the soft leather chair and put one hand on the desk. Her voice was plaintive. "So what am I going to do?"

Mr. Peters leaned back in his high-backed chair. "The new land is the key. If you sell that hundred and sixty acres, you should have enough to pay off the loss on the cattle after you take care of the note on the land. Then, if you sell off all the machinery, as you mentioned earlier, you should take in enough easily to pay the loans on the tractor and combine. You'll have the two hundred and forty free and clear, and you might even be able to sell off the house and buildings as an acreage. That's pretty popular right now for people who work in town.'' He smiled. ''So the total picture isn't really all that grim.''

Katie felt an anger building deep inside. ''Do you know the story about that new land?''

Stanley Peters knew what was coming. He rocked his chair in annoyance. ''This is no time to let sentimentality get in the way of good business sense.''

Katie ignored his remark. ''In 1905, my great-grandfather bought our home place, and his brother bought the hundred and sixty acres right next to it. They lost one of those quarter sections during the Depression, and my great-grandfather died thinking he was a failure because of it. I heard Grandpa Rourke talk about it often enough. Grandpa tried all his life to get that land back, and my father finally managed it eight years ago, and now you're telling me I'm going to lose it again. No, I don't think so!''

Mr. Peters noisily gathered the documents scattered across his desk and stuffed them back into the folder. ''Katie, try to look at this from a business standpoint. You don't have any choice. You can't take in enough money by renting to cover all the outstanding debts. And I don't imagine your teacher's salary will take much of a bite out of all this. Am I right?'' Her silence was answer enough to that question. ''Anyway, this isn't something you've done. The land was already lost.''

She shot an angry look at him. ''You mean you were going to sell out my folks.''

He made eye contact, and his look was calming. ''No, I didn't mean that. We intended to extend the loans. Your mom and dad were good, solid people. This whole county is filled with hardworking folks just like them. We knew your dad would be able to work his way out of all this. I talked with him about it. He knew he was going to have to be a little more careful. I just meant you shouldn't blame yourself in any way whatsoever for losing what I know is an important piece of Rourke heritage. It was all completely beyond your control.''

Katie sat in silence. She wanted to be angry with someone, but common sense told her no one was to blame. The bank had always treated her family fairly. At least her father had always said so. She felt a weakness in her stomach that was just one step from nausea. This, on top of what she had already gone through, was just too much. She had to get out of this place. She had to think all this through. There must be some way around this tangle of debt, short of selling. She stood up abruptly. ''I'm going to have to think all this over. I'll get back to you next week.''

Stanley Peters looked up at her in surprise. He sprang to his feet, but she was already halfway to the door before he could make it around his desk. He fairly ran to open the door for her. ''I'm so sorry to have to bring you such bad news on top of your tragedy.'' He followed her out the door of his office and hurried along at her side. ''Just remember, when you decide what you want to do, I promise you we'll help in any way we can.'' Little did he know he was making a promise he would soon regret.

Katie took the long way home. She turned right from Main onto Parkview and followed the quiet street west by a row of shops that gradually blended into modest homes painted mostly white and set close to the street. Then it was past a sprawling garden center on the right and on the left the Farmer's Elevator with its massive main building thrusting sixty feet into the gray sky and its cluster of once-shiny metal bins neatly lining a short spur of the Illinois Central railroad tracks. In another half mile the smooth pavement gave way to a dusty gravel road, and she could see her destination ahead with its massive wrought-iron fence and rows of dark firs.

She turned into the quiet cemetery and drove less than a hundred feet on the white-rocked road before edging her car onto the snow-crusted grass. She could still see the ruts left by the procession of cars that had parked there little more than a month ago. She left the engine running and got out to stand by the two graves freshly mounded with black soil. She pulled the hood of her jacket up over her head against the raw January day and stood deep in thought long enough for the cold to work its way into her thin boots.

"We need to talk," she said out loud, using the words that had always opened most serious conversations with her folks, going back to when she was a little girl. But now the sound of her own voice startled her. "You used to let me ramble on, and then one of you would always say just the right thing to make sense out of my messed-up brain. I need that now. Oh, how I need it. I'm not about to let them take away the land. Not if I can do anything about it." Suddenly, as the biting wind moaned through the trees around her, whipping oversize flakes of snow through the air, a thought struck her. "That is totally insane," she said shaking her head. "No way could I ever do that. Not alone." She stared unseeing across the landscape of tombstones with names of families she had known all her life, and gave the new idea room to grow. "Or could I?" She hurried back to her car, anxious to get her hands on a calculator to run the numbers. She made a complete circuit of the desolate graveyard and pulled back onto the gravel road.

Katie was so deep in thought as she pulled into the driveway, she almost didn't see the blue pickup parked where it had been the night before. She clinched her jaw, angry at herself for being excited at seeing David Cairn again. *It's about time I get over my first crush,* she thought. As she pulled to a stop, she noticed out of the corner of her eye cigarette smoke curl from the partly opened window on the passenger side of his truck. She turned her head and looked straight into the eyes of a rather strange-looking man looking right back at her. He was sporting several days' growth of beard and lounging lazily in the cab, his white cowboy hat, looking out of place in this farm country, pushed down on his forehead so he could rest his head against the back of the cab.

He sat up, adjusted his hat, and rolled down the window as she got out of the car. "Mornin', ma'am," he drawled. "Sorry if I startled ya. The name's Skibby, Otis Skibby. Dave's new hired help." He held up the burning cigarette. "Dave's inside, but I needed to have me a smoke." He took a drag and the blue smoke whipped out the open window. "And you're Katie Rourke, right? Heard about you. Sorry about your ma and pa. I lost both my folks before I was nineteen. Course, not all at once like you. That must be mighty hard to take."

She smiled at his straightforward words. She guessed him to be not much more than thirty, but his weathered face, especially the deep wrinkles around his pale blue eyes, suggested that they had been thirty tough years. "It hasn't been easy, but friends help a lot."

He nodded. "I expect so. You're lucky that way."

"It was nice meeting you. Did you know you're missing out on a piece of my grandmother's famous apple pie by staying out here in the cold?"

He smiled, showing large, badly stained teeth, and held up the cigarette which had burned dangerously close to his fingers. "I'd just be givin' up one bad habit for another. If lung cancer don't get ya, that there cholesterol will." He smiled and tipped his hat. "You have a nice day, ma'am."

As Katie stepped in the front door, she heard voices from

the kitchen as she expected, and sure enough David Cairn was just finishing a last bite of apple pie as she walked in. "Hello again," she said brightly. She nodded at her grandmother. "I see you remembered the pie this morning?" She turned toward David, folded her arms, and feigned a cross look. "How could you leave that poor man out in the cold while you stuff your face in this nice, warm kitchen?"

He laughed an easy laugh. "So, you've met Otis. I just stepped in for a second. Honest. To see you, actually." Katie raised an eyebrow at this. "How was I to know that Mrs. P was going to tempt me with a piece of her delicious pie?"

Mrs. Pitcher came to his defense. "And I went to the door my own self and invited that young man in, but he said no."

"Grandma," Katie said, "I hate to have to break it to you, but that man seems to care more for his cigarettes than for your pie."

"Well, good riddance to him then," she snorted. "I don't need him smelling up the kitchen."

"He's kind of a character," David said. "He's got a wife and a baby down in Oklahoma. He came up here to visit a cousin and find work. He's planning to bring his family when he gets settled."

"Where are they going to stay?" Katie asked.

David finished the last of his coffee. "I thought I'd put them up at our north place. I've got cattle up there, so I need someone close. Trouble is, the place is kind of a mess. No one's lived in it for over a year."

"Katie and I'd be glad to lend a hand with cleaning, wouldn't we dear?" broke in Mrs. Pitcher.

"Well, sure," answered Katie, wondering what her grandmother was up to.

"I just might take you two up on that offer. And by the way, before I forget what I stopped for." He eyed Katie. "I figured you'd be thinking about renting the farm, and I wanted to put my bid in. I'm in a good position to take on that much extra land. I've got plenty of machinery, and your place is right across the fence, so it would work out great. I promise I'd do a good job for you.''

Grandma Pitcher was beaming. ''I can't think of anyone who would be better. I know your father would approve.''

Katie was still trying to hide her disappointment. This is why he wanted to see me? She slid out a chair and sat down. ''I know you'd do a good job. The thing is, I haven't made up my mind exactly what I plan to do. But I'll let you know for sure when I do decide.''

David's voice now had an edge to it. ''You don't need to be afraid to tell me to my face if you've picked someone else.''

Katie frowned. She didn't like his tone. ''Don't worry. I wouldn't be afraid to tell you to your face. But the simple fact is, I haven't made up my mind what I'm going to do.''

''There isn't a better farmer in the county, I can tell you that,'' said Grandma Pitcher emphatically.

''What's with you two? This is like some kind of tag team match. All right, let me spell it out for you.'' She looked directly at David. ''If I decide to rent the land, you are my number one candidate. Is that clear enough?''

''So, you're thinking about selling, is that it?'' Now he was thinking out loud. ''You'll probably want to auction to get the best money. I'll need to do some serious financing.'' He looked across at her. ''You'll let me in on the bidding, won't you? I don't want to let a good piece of land like this slip away,'' he said emphatically. ''It's every bit as good as my own, and it's right across the fence.''

Katie stood up and crossed her arms. She could feel the heat rise up her neck to her face. ''Who said anything about selling? Selling is the one thing I definitely won't do.'' Then her anger spilled over. ''You seem awfully anxious to get your hands on this land. Is that why you've been hanging around over here? Trying to get my grandmother on your side?''

"Katie!'' Mrs. Pitcher, her hands on her hips, stared at her granddaughter. "How could you say that? David would never do such a thing.''

"Oh, really? Are you sure? Sounds to me like he's got his machinery ready to move across the fence no matter what. Buy or rent, he'll take it either way.''

David stood up quickly. "I know this is a bad time for you, but what you're saying is way, way off base.'' He slipped on his coat and turned to Mrs. Pitcher, who was standing by the counter looking positively stricken at what had just taken place. "I swear, Mrs. P, that isn't why I've been dropping by.''

She took a step toward him and put a hand on his arm. "I didn't think that for a minute,'' she said quietly. "Katie's just upset. She doesn't mean what she's saying.''

Katie glared at the two. "Hello. I'm still in the room. I'm perfectly capable of speaking for myself. All I said was,'' she said, enunciating her words carefully, "Mr. Cairn seems awfully anxious about our land. And it's true; he does.''

David chose not to say anything more. He brushed past her, stalked down the hall and out the door.

Gram sat down heavily in one of the kitchen chairs. "Katie, I'm so ashamed. How could you say that? And to David of all people?'' She shook her head. "It's that Rourke temper, that's what it is.''

Katie was leaning on the back of a chair, her head bowed. She was already regretting her words. And her grandmother was right. Her temper would be the death of her yet. "I'm sorry. You're right. I don't know what came over me. But you will have to admit he sounded awfully grabby.'' Her grandmother glared up at her. "Okay. Okay. No more of those looks, please. I admit I was wrong. I'll go over to his place this very afternoon and apologize.''

She put her hands on her grandmother's shoulders, and the tone in her voice pleaded for forgiveness. "I promise."

She slipped into a chair and studied her grandmother's face. Slowly she reached out and covered one of Gram's hands, resting on the table, with her own. "I'm sorry. Now can we forget about him for two minutes, so you can listen to my wild idea? I've got to tell it to someone, or I'm going to explode." She scratched her head. "Or at least I think it was my idea."

At this, her grandmother looked at her quizzically. "What on earth are you talking about?"

"Oh, you'll see what I mean in a minute. Here, you sit at the table, and I'll grab some paper and a calculator." She scurried into the tiny office next to the kitchen. "I *was* awful, wasn't I? Do you think he'll even let me in the house?" she shouted as she searched her father's rolltop desk for a calculator.

Otis had just lighted a fresh cigarette as David barged out the door and down the porch steps. "Just my luck to fall in with some reformed smoker," he mumbled under his breath. He held the cigarette out the window and snuffed the burning end with a yellowed thumb and forefinger as David climbed in behind the wheel and nearly pulled the door in after him. Otis slipped the cigarette into the pocket of his denim shirt under the worn jeans jacket, straightened his hat, and looked at his new boss. "That's one mighty purty lady if you ask me."

David jerked the truck into reverse and popped the clutch, careening dangerously close to the metal machine shed as he wheeled the pickup around. "She's pretty all right," he said as he yanked the gearshift into first, "but she's got the disposition of a badger." He jammed his foot on the gas, and the truck roared out of the yard and onto the gravel road, with Otis holding his cowboy hat with one hand and the door handle with the other.

Chapter Three

Gram listened closely as her granddaughter told what she had learned from Mr. Peters. Stunned by the unexpected turn of events, she watched Katie, who by this time was already punching the calculator in front of her on the table. "What are we going to do?" the gray-haired woman finally managed.

Her eyes locked on the work in front of her, Katie raised a hand. "Just give me a second here, Gram. I want to see if this will work."

But Gram wasn't about to be put off so easily. She was over her shock now. "And you sent David away? He could help, you know. He'd be the best one to rent to."

Katie looked up from her figuring. "I'm certain you'd be right if we wanted to rent, but that's just the problem. We can't pay off the debt by renting the land because we get only half, and the person doing the farming gets the other half."

Gram's face contorted with a look of confusion. "Then we have to sell?"

Katie pushed the calculator aside and shook her head. "Gram, I can't bring myself to let the land go. I just know Dad and Mom wouldn't want me to. And I think the other Rourkes buried out there in the cemetery feel the same. I stopped there on the way home today, and I could just feel what they wanted me to do." She shook her head as her grandmother rolled her eyes. "I know, I know. It sounds crazy. But you haven't even heard the really crazy part yet. Are you ready for this?'' She watched her grandmother anxiously. "Here goes." She raised a hand and ticked off the options on her fingers. "We can't make enough renting the farm. I don't want to sell it. Sooo . . . what does that leave?''

Her grandmother shrugged her shoulders. "There isn't anything left."

"Oh, yes there is," Katie said with a knowing grin. "We farm it ourselves."

"What?" Gram looked even more confused. "What are you talking about?''

"I'm talking about farming this land all by myself. With your help, of course."

Gram laughed a weak laugh. "You are joking, aren't you?" But seeing the resolute look in Katie's eyes, she swallowed hard. "You farm all this land all by yourself? Out on the tractor and everything? Why, you don't know the first thing about farming."

"That's not true. Remember, I did grow up here. I used to help Dad a lot out in the field."

"Can you drive a tractor and that other big machinery?''

"I used to drive the tractor." She added quickly before her grandmother could interrupt, "Okay, so it's been a few years, but I know I can do it. And I ran Dad's new combine just last fall, and I didn't have any trouble at all."

"But would you know how to get it adjusted and oiled and cleaned or whatever else they do to those things? Your father used to work on those big machines out in front of the shed doing something or other days before he ever went to the field."

Katie had to admit that her grandmother was asking some good questions, and the glitter of her original idea was beginning to dim in the shadow of her own doubt. And Gram wasn't finished yet.

"Do you know when to plant things? And about fertilizer and that chemical they put on the weeds . . . what do they call it?''

''You mean herbicide? I can learn most of what I need to know from reading. Dad's got some books and pamphlets right in there by his desk. And I think I can go to the County Extension Office. Dad used to. I bet they'd help. And you said yourself how good the neighbors are. Maybe even David Cairn will help if he's still talking to me. I've got more than a couple of months before things really start. I can even practice driving the tractor around in the yard here before I have to go to the field for real.'' She was starting to get her confidence back. ''What do you think, Gram? Can we do it?''

Mrs. Pitcher combed her hand through her white hair and shook her head slowly. ''Oh, Katie, I don't know. Do you really know what you're getting into? And what about school? Are you going to give up teaching?''

''The way I've got it figured, it would take just three good years or at the most four to pay off the loans on the cattle and the machinery. Then I think I could rent the land and make enough to pay off the note on the farm. Just three years. I can substitute at school in town here during the winter if I really want to.''

''And what about your gentleman friend back in Rockford? What's he going to say about all this?''

''You mean Steve? That whole thing hasn't been going too well lately. We both pretty much decided to cool it for now.''

''Three years is a long time to cool it, as you young folks say,'' persisted her grandmother.

''No, really, Gram, that's not something to worry about. We're not really serious at all. So, what do you say? Are you with me on this?''

Mrs. Pitcher watched the excitement in her granddaughter's eyes. Here was the old Katie back. The thought had also sneaked into her head while Katie was talking that here was the answer to her prayers too. She wouldn't have to leave her church and her friends and her clubs. At least not for another three or four years, and at this minute, three or four years seemed an eternity away. Was she being selfish, she wondered? Maybe so, but then maybe they could do it. Weren't there lots of women helping their husbands in the field? And she could take care of everything in the house so all Katie had to worry about was the fieldwork. And they had no cattle to cause trouble. Yes, maybe they could do it, she thought. But she still couldn't shake the nagging thought that Katie was doing this all for her. Ruining her own life so an old woman wouldn't have to upset hers. She looked across at her granddaughter, who was waiting for a response. She didn't seem like someone who was ruining her life. The whole venture still seemed crazy, but maybe Katie knew what she was doing. "Well, if you think so," she finally managed.

Katie ignored the doubt in her grandmother's voice. Instead, she jumped to her feet and threw her arms around Gram's neck. "I know we can do it. Now all I have to do is talk Mr. Peters into it." As she spoke, she remembered his promise to help and resolved to hold him to his word. She sat back at the table and tore off the sheet she'd been figuring on. She folded it neatly and slipped it inside the leather flap of the calculator she had been using. She looked up. "Now, just to make you happy, I think I'll run over to David's and apologize. I guess I did get a little carried away."

"Carried away?" Mrs. Pitcher shot her a look of amazement. "I should say so."

"I'm sorry. Sometimes I just see red, and I don't know what's going to come out of my mouth. I wasn't really that bad, was I?"

Mrs. Pitcher patted Katie's hand. "Well, I guess you didn't accuse him of a crime or anything. At least not that I remember."

"Oh, you!" She stood up and headed toward the door. "Well, here goes nothing. The worst he can do is toss me out. Right?" She opened the hall closet and grabbed her coat. "Gram," she shouted back toward the kitchen, "he doesn't have any attack dogs up there, does he?"

She ran out the door and headed for the garage and her dad's pickup. Sugar, lying in the doorway of her doghouse, raised her head when she heard the garage door open. "Hey, girl, want a ride?" Katie called. The dog bounded eagerly to the pickup, hopped in, and took her accustomed place on the passenger's seat. Katie turned left out of the lane, the dog sitting tall next to her, and began the half-mile drive to the Cairn place. She could see the outline of the large white house nestled snugly among the trees. She remembered that dark grove of trees with its nearly hidden buildings as her destination on bike rides as a kid. To her, when she was nine years old, the gentle climb up the gravel road had been a real challenge. Once at the crest of the hill just past the Cairn driveway, she would stop and gasp for breath, looking back at her own red-roofed home nearly hidden by giant cottonwoods. Then, it was back down the hill, coasting almost all the way to her own drive, especially if she kept the wheels on one of the two smooth tracks made by the passing cars and trucks. Once, she remembered, she let her front wheel drift onto the loose gravel by the side of the road and lost control. She remembered picking herself out of a tangle of handlebars and wheels with a badly skinned knee for her mistake. Later, at twelve or thirteen, she could pump up the hill with ease and often made the trip three or four times an evening, hoping to catch just a glimpse of Willow Grove's star forward shooting baskets in front of the garage.

Katie jerked back to the present when she saw his pickup ease out of the drive ahead and come toward her. She rehearsed what she was going to say as she slowed to a stop and rolled down her window. David stopped next to her and leaned out. Katie could see Otis sitting in the passenger seat. His face was in shadow, but she thought she could just make out an amused grin. "Just the person I was on my way to see," David began tentatively. He was squinting his eyes against the bright sky. "I just wanted to set the record straight. I've been thinking about what I said over at your place, and maybe I could have given the impression that I was land-grabbing. Maybe I might have seemed a little overeager. But if I said anything to offend, I'm sorry."

Katie was struck by his sincerity. "Well, what a coincidence. I was just on my way to apologize to you. Gram was about ready to wash my mouth out with soap after you left." Katie ran a hand through her hair to corral it from the wind. "I *did* get kind of carried away. I'm sorry too. You've always been a good friend to my folks."

"Thanks," he said. "I've always felt the same way about them." Their eyes locked and neither said a word for a moment. Otis watched the two with the grin still on his face. The only sound was the idling engines of the pickups. David revved his engine slightly. "Well, I guess that's about all I had to say. If you ever want to talk about the farm or anything like that, you know where to find me. I'd be more than happy to help any way I can."

"Well, thank you," Katie said, obviously touched. "As a matter of fact, I might take you up on that real soon." She smiled broadly, eager to share her news. "I've decided I'm going to farm the land myself, so I'm going to need all the help I can get."

David's jaw dropped and a loud surprised guffaw escaped him even though he tried to stop it. Otis grinned from ear to ear at the turn of events. He was finding his new job most entertaining. "You're going to what?" David asked. He wasn't sure he'd heard correctly.

Katie's eyes had turned steely at the sound of his laughter, and now her lips formed a rigid line. The moment of conciliation was definitely over. "You heard me. I'm going to farm it myself."

"How, may I ask, are you going to do that? You don't know the first thing about farming." He turned his head slightly toward Otis. "Can you believe this? She's going to farm it herself."

Katie could feel the heat again climbing up her neck and onto her face despite the chilling wind gusting through the open window. "What's so funny about that?" she blurted. "I grew up on a farm, didn't I? I ought to know something about it." She started to roll up her window, but stopped suddenly. "I can tell you one thing. Nobody's going to take this place away from me if I have anything to do with it." She dropped the gearshift into drive and pressed her foot to the floor. The pickup fishtailed slightly as it sped up the hill, kicking up a hail of gravel that pelted the back of David's pickup. Sugar lost her balance and dropped to a crouching position next to Katie.

"Whooee," Otis shouted. "That little gal's got a temper." David barely heard his hired man. As he eased the pickup into gear and continued slowly down the road, he wondered, *Why is she so worried about someone taking away the land?* He shook his head. *She's making one big mistake if she thinks she can raise a crop by herself. She's too delicate. Anyone can see that.*

Chapter Four

Katie waited two full days before making another appointment with Mr. Peters at the bank. Gram had said they should sleep on this idea of hers, so they slept on it for two nights for good measure. Mr. Peters was waiting at his desk with the ominous folder and a written agenda of what needed to be done to put an auction of the land and machinery into motion. He even had the names and phone numbers of half a dozen eager and successful farmers in the area who should be given special notification of any sale plans. David Cairn's name headed the list. He greeted Katie warmly as before, ushered her to a chair, and then sat dumbfounded as she eagerly outlined her plan.

"So, Mr. Peters," she finished breezily, "what I need is the transfer of the notes on the land, the machinery, and the cattle to my name for a one-year period. I plan to renew them each year until they're paid off. My timetable calls for the clearing of the cattle and machinery notes in three years. Then I hope to handle the remainder of the farm loan by renting out the land as I originally planned. You had already made a similar agreement with my father, so I assume the same will apply to me. Oh, and I may need to borrow enough to get my crop in the ground this spring. There's more than enough for that in the estate, but I'm not sure it will be probated in time." She smiled sweetly at him and folded her hands in her lap.

Mr. Peters fell back in his chair and stared at this fragile-looking young woman for a long minute until he found his voice again. "You aren't joking, are you?"

"No, I assure you I'm not joking."

"But, do you know the first thing about farming?"

"Of course I do. I grew up on a farm, didn't I?"

"Well, yes," he stammered, "but there's a world of difference between growing up on a farm and farming it yourself."

"I'm planning to use the months before fieldwork starts familiarizing myself with the machinery and reading as much as I can."

Mr. Peters leaned forward and stared at Katie. He couldn't keep his voice from betraying his doubt. "You mean to tell me you're going to learn everything there is to know about farming in the next three months from books?"

"Right. Well, not everything there is to know. No one can learn everything there is to know about farming even in a lifetime. I know Dad was still learning."

There was another long silence. This time when he spoke, Mr. Peters sounded as if he were talking to a child. "Katie, I think the bank would feel more comfortable with a . . . how shall I put it . . . more certain conclusion to these loans."

Katie had planned her words carefully in advance. "Mr. Peters, it seems to me the bank is under no risk here. I'm the one assuming the risk, wouldn't you agree? The home place secures all of these loans, doesn't it?"

"Well, yes, that's true."

"And the value of that farm more covers the amounts owed on the loans, right?"

He nodded. "Yes, that's true also."

"So, why should the bank feel uncomfortable, as you put it?" She couldn't keep a hint of sarcasm from slipping into her voice. "Of course, I'll admit the bank will lose the percentage for handling a land sale and a machinery auction.''

Mr. Peters shifted uncomfortably in his chair. ''Now, Katie, I don't think that's a fair way of looking at it. I assure you we're not trying to take advantage of your personal tragedy. Believe me, we're concerned about you. You could lose a lot of money on this wild plan. Think what could happen if you don't get a crop out this year. You stand to lose everything.''

''And I've decided that if I can't keep all the Rourke land as my father intended, then it doesn't make any difference if I lose it all.'' At the pained look on his face, she added quickly, ''Not that I intend to. I know I can raise a crop.''

Mr. Peters sat with his chin resting on a closed fist, his elbow propped on the arm of the chair. ''I really question whether the bank can get involved in such an arrangement.''

Katie leaned forward. She was ready with her trump card. ''Mr. Peters, just the other day in this very office you promised to help in any way you could. This is something I've got to try. The risk is all mine, and believe me, I know what I'm getting into.''

''Oh, Katie, I don't think you really do know what you're getting into. How can you possibly handle all this even from a physical standpoint?''

''I'm a lot stronger than I look.''

He shook his head slowly. ''I think you're going to regret this. And old C. W. will skin me alive when he reviews the deal. But you're right, I did promise.'' He shook his finger at Katie. ''That wasn't fair to throw a promise back at me, young lady. Okay, I must be as crazy as you are, but you've got your extension.''

Katie sighed deeply and smiled across the desk. ''And the extra loan for this year's crop?''

''You don't give up, do you?'' He bit his lip. ''Okay,

okay, that too. I guess you've got to have seed and fertilizer.''

"Thank you,'' she said. ''I know this is going to work
out.''

"I hope you're right. Now, remember,'' he added
quickly, ''this is only for one year, and then we review
before we go to a second.'' Katie nodded in agreement.
''I'll have the papers drawn up, and we'll have them ready
for your signature tomorrow. He looked at his watch. About
this time? Will that work for you?'' He smiled. ''That is
if I'm still here when C. W. gets wind of all this.'' He stood
and reached across the desk to shake hands. Her grip was
a strong one. *She's going to need all of that and more for
what she's bitten off,* he thought to himself.

"Gram, I'm home'' Katie shouted as she slammed the
door behind her.

"In here, dear,'' Gram called from the living room.

Katie hung up her coat and joined her grandmother. She
couldn't hide her excitement. ''It was a struggle, but he
finally gave in. I have to sign the papers tomorrow.''

Gram set her sewing aside and studied her granddaughter. She had spent the morning worrying. Worrying first
that Mr. Peters would say no, and then worrying that he
would say yes. ''Are you sure you're doing the right
thing?''

Katie dropped into a chair. ''I hope so. Anyway it's too
late now.''

"You still have time to change your mind if you haven't
signed anything.''

"My mind's made up,'' Katie assured her. ''I know I
can do this. With your help, of course.''

Grandma sighed, wondering what part her own selfish-
ness had played in Katie's decision. Of course, it would be
nice not to have to pick up what was left of her life and
start over hundreds of miles away. She had thought that all

out this morning. But at what cost? She felt suddenly very old. Help indeed! Of what possible help could an old lady like her be at a time like this? She had already been excess baggage to a daughter and son-in-law for three years. Bless their souls, they never let on. And now she was picking up where she'd left off, about to ruin the life of the dearest person left to her on this earth. Well, it wasn't too late to talk some sense into this granddaughter of hers. She cleared her throat. "I don't know, dear. Maybe this isn't such a good idea." Gram's tone took Katie by surprise. "I guess I've been kind of an old fool about not wanting to move away. It might be kind of fun to start over in Illinois. Mind you, in my own little apartment. I wouldn't want to be underfoot. Anyway, this farming business has been fun to dream about, but actually doing it . . . now that's another thing altogether."

Katie sat in disbelief at this sudden change of heart. She studied her grandmother closely until the truth hit home. "Oh, now I get it. You think I want to do this so you won't have to move away. Right?" Gram inspected her hands resting in her lap. "I thought so. That's just what you were thinking, isn't it?" She leaned forward. "Okay, I'll admit that thought did enter my head, but it's not the main reason I want to do this. I was going to wheedle you into coming back to Illinois with me anyway, and I'll bet you wouldn't find it half bad." She bowed her head to collect her thoughts. "Gram, I know this seems crazy. It even seemed kind of crazy when I was telling Mr. Peters. But I've just got to try to keep the land. Maybe it sounds corny, but it's my only link to the past. If I let it go, I lose everything that went before me." She shook her head slowly. "Like great-grandpa Rourke and his brother that I never even knew, but somehow I feel like I know them." She looked up and met her grandmother's eyes. "Does that make any sense, or am I going completely crazy?"

Her grandmother smiled. No, dear, you're not going

crazy. I think I understand." The little, gray-haired woman suddenly felt lighter than air. A weight had just been lifted from her. She knew now that Katie wanted to stay. Not just because of an old woman. She smiled to herself. No, because of people dead and buried, some a long time. Esther Pitcher breathed deeply. She squared her shoulders. Yes, now she had a new reason to crawl out of bed in the morning. She knew she could help. Oh, not in any physical way, she understood that. But she could be there for Katie. She looked at the strong face across from her, the eyes so bright and alive, and knew she had never been prouder of her granddaughter than she was at this moment, and that was saying something. "I think we can do it, dear," she whispered. And then with a stronger voice, she added, "I think we can do it together."

Chapter Five

The next morning, when Katie came to the kitchen for breakfast, her grandmother was knee-deep in cleaning supplies—literally knee-deep. She had buckets and mops and brooms and various bottled and canned cleaning supplies piled on the floor. Katie had to step around the pile on her way to the refrigerator. Grandma was making a racket as she tried to pull the upright Hoover from its storage place deep in the recesses of the hall closet. Katie went to the kitchen door and peered down the hall. "What in the world is going on around here?"

Gram rolled the vacuum toward the front door and then came back into the kitchen mopping her brow. "Just getting ready for the big cleaning day."

Katie stopped with the juice carton in one hand and turned slowly to study her grandmother suspiciously. "What cleaning day might that be?"

"Remember, today's the day we help David and that hired man of his fix up the north place."

Katie put the juice container down heavily on the counter and a splash of orange juice shot out the top. "No, as a matter of fact I don't remember anything of the sort."

Gram rubbed her chin with a forefinger and tried to look surprised, confused, and innocent all at the same time. "I must have forgotten to tell you. I called him while you were at the bank and set it all up."

"Well, you can just unset it all up. After the way he

acted? No way am I going to help him.'' She filled her juice glass, aware that her grandmother was carrying the cleaning supplies to the front door. She waited until Gram came back for more. ''Did you hear what I said? I'm not going to lift a finger to help that . . . that self-centered, arrogant creep.''

''But, dear, I promised, and I won't go back on a promise. So I'm going to help if I have to walk there myself. And if you won't do it for David, think about Otis and his wife and little one. They need our charity.''

Katie gritted her teeth. She knew she was going to lose this one. ''You're up to something. I can always tell when you get that little smirky look.''

Grandma put her hands on her hips in exaggerated indignation. ''I don't know what you're talking about.''

Katie pointed. ''There it is right now. That smirky look. You're up to something all right.'' She was pouring Wheaties, and ran the flakes over the bowl and onto the counter. She stamped her foot. ''All right, I'll go, but I'm not going to talk to him.''

Gram smiled in victory. ''Thank you, dear. I knew I could count on you.''

Katie glanced at her grandmother as she cleaned up the counter. It was good to see her showing some spunk, but she could be maddening at times. She waved her hand toward the cleaning supplies. ''Do we really need all this stuff?''

''Well, no one's touched that house for ages. We need to be prepared.''

''I'd say we're prepared all right.'' Katie popped a piece of bread into the toaster. ''I guess we'd better take the pickup. I don't think we can get all this in the car.''

Katie backed the pickup out of the machine shed and maneuvered it as close to the back porch as possible. It took her four trips to get everything into the red Ford. She slammed the tailgate and pulled down and latched the door of the aluminum topper that was mounted over the back of the truck. She helped her grandmother with the high first step into the cab, climbed in herself, and they were off. Katie drove slowly past David's place, but there was no sign of the blue pickup. She drove on toward the next grove of trees off in the distance, a grove that looked much smaller than she remembered. She knew this farm had once belonged to a couple named Anderson, and she vaguely recalled that the Cairns had bought it a number of years earlier. Maybe ten years ago, she thought. She guessed that David's dad had expanded probably when David finished college.

As she drew nearer, she could see why everything looked so different to her. The barn and most other outbuildings were gone. All that was left was the small one-story house and a large garage with a double-wide overhead door that was open now, with David's pickup parked in front of it. She could see the remains of the past season's cornstalks, and it was obvious that the rows encroached on what had once been a farmstead that she knew had held a large barn, a corncrib, a machine shed, a hog house, a chicken coop, and a fenced lot for feeding cattle and hogs. When she saw the house, it suddenly dawned on her that it wasn't terribly old, not more than fifteen years, which probably explained why it hadn't been torn down. Yes, now she remembered. Mr. Anderson built it for his wife. Then he died of a heart attack no more than three years later, and Mrs. Anderson left the farm and moved to town.

This wouldn't be a bad spot for Otis and his family, she thought as she pulled to a stop. That is, if they could get some kind of space between the house and the field. David's farming led practically up to the front door. At least he had left some of the trees on the north to give the house some protection. *I suppose that's where he keeps the cattle he was talking about,* thought Katie. With a look of resignation firmly set on her face, she joined her grandmother to take what they could carry from the back of the truck and climbed the two steps to a stoop that led, by a metal storm door, into an enclosed porch with windows on three sides.

"This would be nice for sitting out in the summer," remarked Mrs. Pitcher.

"Maybe so, but not today. It's freezing out here," said Katie as she set down the vacuum and opened the plain wooden door that led into a spacious kitchen. The pair stepped inside and surveyed the dismal surroundings. The cold, gray day outside did nothing to brighten the room, and when Katie flicked the switch just inside the door, nothing happened. She shivered. "It's not much warmer in here. Matter of fact, it's not *any* warmer in here. What gives? No lights? No heat?" Her mood, low enough already at the prospect of trying to be pleasant to the man who had laughed in her face, was sinking still lower.

"Anybody here?" shouted Gram close to Katie's ear.

Katie jerked her head away. "Gee, Gram, easy on the eardrum."

"We're down here," came a voice beneath them. "Be right up."

Suddenly the overhead light came on, and the refrigerator began to whir noisily.

"Let there be light," said Grandma with a smile. "We'll have this place shipshape in no time."

Katie looked at the cobwebs hanging from the ceiling and the layer of dust coating the counter and the ground-in grime on the linoleum floor, and shook her head. "I think this ship has already sunk."

They heard the thud of footsteps on the stairs and the low murmurs of two voices and turned toward an open door on the far side of the kitchen, where the sounds were coming from. David and Otis appeared, each carrying a flashlight, and David had a large metal toolbox in one hand. He set the toolbox on the floor and smiled at the two women. It was easy to see by Katie's stony look that she was still upset about the other day. There was a frost in the air, and not just because of the January day and the lack of heat in the house. "Good morning," he said with forced cheerfulness. "Think we can make this place livable?"

Before they had a chance to answer, Otis cleared his throat. "I'm obliged to you two kind ladies for helpin' out," he said, looking like a schoolboy giving a speech. "I want to pretty this place up for my Becky, but I don't know how to do that. I guess you'd say I'm kinda all thumbs when it comes to stuff like that. You know Becky and me ain't had much since we been married, and I'd like to make it up to her somehow. This place here'll go a long way to doin' it." Otis's face flushed when he realized how much he had really said. He hung his head and stuffed his hands in his back pockets.

Katie suddenly felt a weight of guilt for the attitude she had carried through the door a few minutes ago. She took a fresh look at the room and tried to see it through the eyes of Otis's Becky. "We'll have this place shining in no time," she said. "I'll bet Gram can whip up some curtains, and we might even be able to slap on some paint to give it a fresh look." Grandma Pitcher tried her best to hide a smile at this about-face when she caught Katie's eye, but she did raise her eyebrows so high that her wire-rim glasses came completely off the bridge of her nose.

I know what you're thinking, Katie tried to say back with her eyes when she saw the smug look on her grandmother's face, *but I'm doing this for Otis, not for him.*

David thought he was sensing a thaw in the air. "We got the gas and the electricity turned on, and we lit the pilot lights on the furnace and the water heater." He stepped past the two women into the next room. "Let's turn up the thermostat and see if we can make things a little more comfortable." He fiddled with the dial. "There we go. The fan'll kick on in a minute, and this place will be toasty before you know it.'' He returned to the kitchen. ''Now,'' he said, rubbing his hands together, ''what do you want us to do? Your wish is our command.''

Mrs. Pitcher laughed, but Katie showed no expression. ''Well, I guess to start with,'' said Mrs. Pitcher, ''you could get the rest of the things out of the truck. Then we'll divide up chores.'' The two men filed out the door, and Grandma picked up one of the plastic buckets they had brought and headed for the kitchen sink. ''Let's see if the water is hot enough yet to do some scrubbing.'' She slipped the bucket under the faucet and turned the handle. The faucet let out a blast of air that made her jump back a few steps in surprise. She returned to the sink warily as the faucet spit and gasped. Katie peered over her shoulder. Finally, a stream of dark, rusty water spurted into the bucket.

''Yuck,'' Katie shrieked. ''How are we going to clean anything with that?'' She and her grandmother watched as the bucket filled with the brown ooze.

The kitchen door opened, and the two men trooped in loaded down with cans and bottles, mops and buckets. ''What's the trouble?'' asked David as he set his load down on the floor.

''Just look at this water,'' said Katie. ''It's gross.''

He stepped closer and dipped his hand in the bucket. ''Just some sediment,'' he said in a flat tone of voice. ''Probably from the water heater. Let it run awhile, and it'll clear.''

Katie stepped away from the sink and sniffed the air. ''What's that disgusting smell?'' She looked back at the bucket. ''Is that the water?''

David forced a laugh. ''No, no, that's the furnace. The fan just came on. It smells that way because it hasn't been used for a long time.''

She looked around the room and put her hands on her hips. Her frustration bubbled over. ''I don't think this place is fit to live in. Who knows, that furnace could blow up any minute, and this water looks like it came out of a sewer. If you tried to rent a place like this in the city, they'd have you arrested.''

David turned on her angrily. His face was flushed. ''I don't know how they do things in the city, but I'm telling you all this place needs is a good fixing up. And no one's begging you to help. Otis and I are perfectly capable of taking care of it.''

''Would you two stop your bickering,'' Grandma said sharply, just as Katie was opening her mouth to fire off another round. ''I swear, you're worse than a couple of schoolkids. Now are you two going to help out here or are Otis and I going to have to do it all ourselves?''

David and Katie stood glaring at each other, their faces rigid.

Otis cleared his throat. ''Why don't we just leave it be for right now? I can do some of the heavy scrubbin' in the evenin's, and then Becky and me can finish up when she gets here next week. I don't wanta be the cause a no fightin' between you folks.''

Katie looked away from David and dumped the bucket of brown water into the sink. She turned on the faucet to let the water run clear. ''All right, what do you want me to do?'' she asked in a tone of resignation.

''Don't do us any favors,'' David said. ''I told you we can do it ourselves.''

''I said I'd help, and I'll help.'' She looked at her grandmother and spoke more quietly. ''I'll do the windows. Okay?''

''Honestly, you two!'' Grandma rummaged through the pile of supplies on the floor and gave Katie a bottle of Windex and a roll of paper towels. ''Otis, what're we going to do with this pair? I guess we just have to keep them separated.''

*   *   *

Katie was working in the back bedroom, the master bedroom. She was on the second window and was cleaning
the dust from the wood trim and sills for good measure.
She could hear the muffled voices of Gram and Otis, who
had taken the main bathroom as their challenge. Gram's
specialty was bringing lost sinks back to their porcelain
brilliance, and her apprentice was trying to work the same
magic with the tub, following her expert advice. Though
she couldn't hear a word they were saying, Katie could
easily distinguish their voices—Otis's low-pitched drawl
and Grandma's gentle, songlike tone.

Working alone as she was, with only her own thoughts
to keep her company, Katie was already feeling guilty for
her outburst. She glanced around. Nothing wrong with this
room, she thought. She had gone through a large living
room to get to this bedroom and was surprised to see that
both were fully carpeted with what looked like quality stuff.
This place isn't so bad, she thought, as she gave the glass
a second spritz of Windex. *I've been a real brat. I swear,
sometimes my mouth just runs on all by itself. Well, he
started it anyway.* She smiled. *That sounds familiar. Just
like being back at good old Herreman High.* She tilted her
head to catch her reflection in the window. *Okay, what say
we try to be a little more civil? That is, unless he starts
something.*

David was alone in the kitchen attacking the grimy linoleum with a squeeze-top foam mop and a bucket of hot
water laced with Mr. Clean. He was scrubbing furiously,
taking out his anger on a trail of footprints leading from
the kitchen door. *What is it with that woman? What does
she think I am, some kind of slumlord?* He surveyed the
room. *This place doesn't look half bad to me.* His eyes
rested on the refrigerator. *Well, maybe that ought to go. It
is noisy. Might keep the baby up at night. Probably as old*

as the house anyway. He squeezed the mop head into the sink, watching the grimy water run down the drain.

He dunked the mop into the bucket of water and started again by the stove. This time, his scrubbing strokes were much calmer. *That rusty water heater down in the basement worries me. I think we could put in a new one ourselves. While we're at it, might as well have the furnace checked. No sense in taking any chances. It hasn't been used for a while.* He squeezed the mop again into the sink, slipped the nearly empty bucket under the faucet, and turned it on. He stared out the window at the gray day. *Damn, she's something when she gets steamed. Red face. Red hair.* He smiled at the image in his head, but sobered quickly when he remembered her anger was aimed solely at him. *Why me? Yeah, like I don't know. She's still doing a burn about that business on the road the other day. I wish I could learn to keep my big mouth shut. I didn't mean to laugh. It just slipped out. The thought of somebody as beautiful as she is up there in a tractor cab just cracks me up.* He turned off the water and hoisted the bucket out of the sink. *Who knows, maybe she can hack it. She's about as gritty as any woman I've ever laid eyes on. One thing's for sure. Joan could never do it. Not in a million years.* He laughed to himself at the thought of his ex-wife sitting in a tractor seat. She might get her hands dirty. He opened the bottle of Mr. Clean and poured in a fresh dose. *I could help her. Just to get started. Yeah, like that would ever happen. She'd snap my head off if I even so much as offered.*

Katie was putting the finishing touches on the second of four windows in the living room when David dragged the upright Hoover through the front door from the porch where he'd left it. He suspended the tank with one hand and held the hose with the other while he took careful steps across the linoleum he had just scrubbed, trying to find the dry spots. He set the vacuum down with a clatter just inside the living room door. Katie looked around with a start at the racket, and their eyes met. She willed her lips to smile, but wasn't sure what the finished result was. He nodded stiffly in her direction, and then dropped to his knees to plug in the vacuum. The roar from the machine took over, and he began to push-pull slowly from the kitchen door to the center of the room. Katie picked up her Windex and roll of towels and moved to the third window. She did her first pass with cleaner and paper towel, and stepped back to see what part of the window needed more work just as David moved backward in his push-pull motion with the Hoover. They bumped hard, and both turned around in surprise. He clicked off the vacuum. "Sorry," he said awkwardly. "I'll wait till you're through in here."

"No, that's okay," she answered quickly. "I'm almost done. You can go ahead."

Gram bustled into the room just at that moment, with Otis right behind. She was wearing bright yellow rubber gloves, holding them away from her body as if she'd been handling toxic waste. "What's going on out here? Otis, look, they're in the same room, and no one's been maimed, as far as I can see."

"Oh, stop it," Katie said, with an embarrassed look on her face.

"But have you been getting any work done?" Gram asked. She walked toward the windows and looked them up and down. "Not bad. We need to do the outside when it warms up." She walked past the three of them toward the kitchen. Katie rolled her eyes as Gram poked her head in and looked around. "That floor is clean enough to eat off of." She looked at David. "But you didn't do the counter and the cabinets first, like I said. When you do them, you're going to mess up your pretty floor."

"Sorry. Guess I wasn't thinking straight. I'm so starved I can't get my brain to work right." He looked at the others. "Isn't anyone else hungry?" he asked, and he couldn't keep the pleading out of his voice. "I didn't have time for breakfast this morning. How about I run into town and bring back some pizza?"

"You men," said Grandma Pitcher. "All you ever think about is your stomachs." She began peeling off the rubber gloves. "I guess I could force something down," she said with a smile. "How about you two?" She looked at Otis and Katie, and they nodded their approval.

A slow thaw began over pizza, but it was more like an arctic summer—not enough heat to melt all the ice. "I swear, you two are the stubbornest pair I've ever laid eyes on," said Gram that evening at home. "Neither one of you'll budge an inch."

"That's not true, Gram. We talk," Katie protested.

"Oh, sure, like a couple of robots." She stood stiffly with her arms straight at her sides and her eyes staring straight ahead. "Cold weather we're having lately," she parodied.

Katie laughed weakly. "Oh, come on now. We're not that bad." But she confessed to herself that they were. There was an awkwardness between them that just wouldn't go away. They had both said things they couldn't take back. And he had laughed at her. She seethed inside every time she thought about it.

And their silliness, as Gram called it, went on for another two days. That's how long the cleanup took. Gram packed a lunch those next two days—sandwiches and chips and cookies. The second day, she even made up some potato salad. They ate in the kitchen, sitting on the floor since there was no furniture. Gram preferred a folding chair which she'd found in one of the closets. She carried the conversation in the chilly atmosphere, and she didn't get much help from Otis. Oh, he certainly wasn't angry at anyone. Quite the opposite. He could see some good things happening in his life for a change. The trouble was, as far as Gram could tell, he just wasn't the chatty type. That's why the bomb he dropped on them the second day at lunch was so surprising.

It started when Katie mentioned something she'd seen on television the night before about bungee jumping and said she'd like to try it. Grandma Pitcher snorted and said anybody'd be crazy to trust their life to a skinny rubber band. Katie argued that some people say you have to risk life to really appreciate it. And the words were scarcely out of her mouth when Otis made one of his rare observations. "Whoever said that said a mouthful," he blurted. "I ain't never felt more alive than when some ugly bull was tap-dancin' on my face."

The other three stopped in mid bite and stared at the Oklahoma cowboy. "You mean to tell me you're a bull-fighter?" asked Gram.

Otis grinned shyly. "Well, kinda, ma'am. But not the kind that wears those tight pants and waves a cape. I was a rodeo clown."

They all pressed him for more, and he, in his slow drawl, reluctantly provided some details. He had clowned for a major rodeo circuit in the Southwest for five seasons. Then, just two years ago, at the start of his sixth season, he moved in too close to a bull, trying to get him away from the cowboy he'd just thrown. The bull caught him at mid ring before he could reach the safety of his barrel, and the way Otis put it, "he bullyragged me pretty good afore they could get him off."

"Were you hurt bad?" asked Gram as she laid a hand on his arm. Embarrassed by all this attention, Otis told in a voice so low the three had to lean toward him to hear that he had been laid up for six months recovering, and he knew his rodeo days were over for good. Katie knew now the key to this man. As she watched his eyes brighten at the memory of his rodeo days, and then cloud again as the reality returned to him that those best days were gone forever, she let herself hope that life in Willow Grove might just prove him wrong. She looked across at her grandmother, who had turned her gentle eyes on this rough cowboy sitting on the floor next to her, and thought if anyone could make him turn from the past to the future, she was the one.

Hadn't that wonderful woman already agreed to Katie's wild scheme to farm the land? And what about this house? Hadn't she worked magic with it? Look what they had done in four days. Sure, she knew Gram had a big heart. She'd seen lots of examples of that before. And she even knew Gram could work people half her age into the ground. But she'd never seen her take over like she had these past few days. Why, you could even call her bossy. Yes, the house had made Katie see her grandmother as she had never really seen her before. She seemed to find something new that needed their attention even before they had finished their last project. They painted two full rooms, including the ceilings. They scrubbed the insides of the kitchen cabinets and put down contact paper. They rented a steam cleaner and attacked all of the carpeting in the house. She insisted a broken pane of glass in the spare bedroom be replaced. She was unhappy with the leaky faucets in the bathroom and wanted them repaired. When the sun came out, she had both men outside scrubbing windows. Katie laughed inside every time she saw Gram order David around. She knew he was used to giving orders, not taking them. But she had to admit he took it well. Such was his respect for Gram, Katie felt certain that if she asked him to jump off the roof of the house, he would run off to get a ladder.

All this painting and scrubbing and cleaning was good for Katie. It took her mind off her worries. She knew she had to face the future and start her self-imposed crash course, but that could wait until next week. For the time being, she would just work herself into a satisfying state of exhaustion. The first evening, Katie dozed peacefully in front of the television, only vaguely aware that her grand-mother was up to something. She padded into the kitchen in her floppy slippers once to see what was going on. Gram hadn't changed from her grubby khaki slacks and paint-spattered sweatshirt. She was sitting at the kitchen table with the telephone directory spread out in front of her. She had the receiver in one hand and was sliding a finger down the page of names.

"What on earth are you doing?" Katie asked.

"Oh, just never you mind," she replied. "You'll know soon enough."

Katie shook her head and wandered sleepily back to the living room. And sure enough, the next day, out at the house, she found out what Gram had been up to. It started about nine-thirty. Neighbors from miles around began drift-ing by, most of them in pickup trucks, to drop off pieces of used but very serviceable furniture for Otis's new home. Grandma showed no surprise at the deliveries, and she knew exactly where each item belonged, as if she'd ordered it. She always invited the folks in for coffee and cookies she had somehow managed to bake the night before. Otis had his hand shaken and was welcomed more times than Katie could remember that day. And she noticed that he never seemed comfortable with the generosity of people he had never laid eyes on. As more furniture appeared during the day, the house began to look more like a home.

And then the work was done. Katie had just finished loading the buckets and mops and cleaning supplies. She had the vacuum waiting by the door. David and Otis trooped up from the basement, where they had just installed a new water heater. "It looks better than it did when we walked in," Gram said emphatically.

"You can say that again," Katie added.

"There's still some finishing up to do, but we're going to leave some for Becky," Gram said. She looked at Otis.

"She should have her say about curtains and such, but I'll be more than happy to help when she's made up her mind," she added, with a hand on his shoulder.

He smiled back sheepishly at her, trying to thank her with a look. "You've done a mighty lot already. I swear we couldn't a done it without you." He held his hand out awkwardly to shake hers. "Dang me if Becky ain't gonna be surprised."

Katie stole a look at David, only to discover to her surprise that he was intently studying *her*. Her face reddened, and she glanced quickly away.

"Otis is right," he said evenly. "We couldn't have done all this without you two. I mean it."

Chapter Six

Katie dragged herself out of bed the next morning with a vague feeling of emptiness. The weather had turned bitterly cold. The January thaw was over, and the forecast was for snow, possibly lots of it. But she knew she couldn't blame her feelings on the change in the weather. The work of the past few days had given her a sense of direction. She didn't mind taking orders from her grandmother because she didn't have to make the decisions herself. But she couldn't expect her grandmother to continue to shoulder the load in what was to come. Katie had made up her own mind to farm the land, and it was high time she got to it. She had been able to drift during the past few days, and maybe that was just what she needed. But drifting was over. Now it was time to make serious plans.

After breakfast, she settled into her father's office, just next to the kitchen. She sat in his swivel chair in front of the big rolltop desk for a few moments and then started to sort through the papers, pamphlets, and magazines stacked neatly on one side of the desk. She spotted his well-worn loose-leaf notebook and paged through it slowly. A plot map caught her eye. She recognized the clear designation of the various fields that made up their land. Her land now, she thought with a sudden weight of responsibility. She noted where her father had penciled, in his firm hand, the crops for the past year, alternating between corn and beans, the cash crops of choice in most of the state. Or were those his plans for the coming year? She tried to remember what crops had grown in what fields this past summer, but had to admit she really hadn't noticed.

Well, no matter, she could check those fields herself, but she'd better do it today. There was snow on the way, if you could believe the weatherman. She stared off the page. *I could ask David,* she thought. Events of the past few days flashed through her mind. *Then again, maybe not. Gram was right. We never really did talk about anything during all that time. It would have been a good time to ask some questions. And whose fault was that? Okay, probably most of it was mine. I sure didn't make it any easier for him. And I really tried to avoid him. But every time he looks at me, I just know what's going through his head. He thinks I'm going to screw up. And he's just waiting around to watch it happen.* Then, without warning, she saw again (no, felt rather than saw) his eyes studying her from across Otis's kitchen, and the heat slowly crept up her neck to her cheeks all over again. *What is going on here,* she asked herself. She held her face in her hands for a few seconds and forced herself back to the here and now.

Okay, where was I? What was planted where? She scratched her head. *What difference does it make anyway? I'm going to plant all corn. Dad wouldn't like that, would he? He liked alternating between corn and beans. But I can make more money with corn. I've got to make as much as possible the first year to convince Mr. Peters and the bank that they made a good deal. I should ask David what he thinks.* She wrinkled her nose. *There I go again.* She sighed aloud. *If I could just climb on the tractor and go out to the field and do what has to be done, I know I could handle it. But it's all of these maddening details: When to work the field? How much seed corn to buy? Where to buy it? How much fertilizer? What kind of fertilizer?* She remembered Gram's same questions and her own glib answers.

Somehow it didn't seem quite so simple now that the first flush of excitement at doing such a wild thing had worn off. Her head was spinning. *I wonder if I could ask him. Oh, right, he's going to love answering a bunch of stupid questions. And anyway, why should I give him the satisfaction of knowing he was right in the first place?*

She placed her father's notebook gently, almost reverently, on the desk, and went back to the kitchen. There, for several long minutes, she stared vacantly out the window at the bare trees being shaken by a north wind that had ushered in the coldest weather of the winter so far. She stuck her head into the living room, where her grandmother was bent over her stitchery, the television tuned to some talk show. "I'm going out to the machine shed to check things over."

Gram looked up from her work. "In weather like this? You put your heavy coat on and a hat, young lady. I just heard them say the windchill is five below."

"Okay, Gram," she shouted from the hall closet, feeling just like a child again, told to bundle up to meet the bus. She pulled on her heavy coat, drew the hood up over her head, and reached in the pockets for her warm mittens. She stepped out the door and headed toward the metal machine shed, hunching her shoulders against the cold as the full force of the wind caught her from behind. Sugar darted from the doghouse to trot at her side, glad for some company on such a day. Katie reached out a mittened hand to pat the shaggy head, then fumbled for the drawstrings on her jacket to pull the hood tighter, to keep the biting wind from finding her ears. She jogged heavily the last thirty feet. Her thin sweatpants and low-cut tennis shoes weren't designed for such arctic weather.

She opened the solid metal door next to the closed giant overhead one and stepped inside. She groped for the light switch mounted on the corrugated metal wall and flicked it on. The huge building was suddenly bathed in light from three oversize bulbs, protected by green reflectors and dangling from the ceiling. It wasn't much warmer inside the big unheated building, but at least she was protected from the strong north wind. She took a few steps, her shoes kicking up tiny clouds of dust from the dry dirt floor. She pushed the hood off her head and craned her neck to see everything. She smiled. It was all green—from the tractors to the combine to the plow. Her dad loved anything John Deere, and that included the cap he was never without.

She left the door open, and walked a few steps down a narrow alleyway between the combine, its bean head still in place, parked next to the mud-splattered tractor. Sugar watched her curiously, then curled up by the wheel of the combine, where she could keep an eye on things. The machinery was parked in the reverse order of its use. She imagined that her father had just driven the combine inside the door after he had finished the beans, and there it sat. She remembered the weather had turned rainy in late October, and he hadn't gotten the beans combined until the last week of November.

As she looked from one huge machine to another, she shivered, but not from the cold. The stark reality of what she was planning was really sinking in. She could see the planter parked near the back of the shed, its two row-markers pointed skyward. The second tractor was nestled in just to the side of the combine. She saw a disk, its rows of shiny, circular blades reflecting the light from the ceiling. And there was a chisel plow that she had to admit she had never even seen used. As her eyes moved from one piece of equipment to another, the awful truth hit her. She didn't know a darned thing about how to use most of these machines. *Let's face it,* she thought, *I don't even know how to hitch most of them to the tractor. I must have been out of my mind when I came up with this harebrained idea.*

She was standing next to the tractor, and she kicked the big tire out of frustration. The tire was hard, and her toe cold. "Damn," she cried out loud as she hopped on one foot and brought the other up to try to massage the hurt toe through her tennis shoe. The dog sprang to her side at the sound of her voice and stood staring up at her. "No, not you, Sugar. I wasn't talking to you." She leaned against the tire, cradling her foot clumsily, and stared at all the machinery around her. And then something strange happened. She began to feel better about it all for no good reason that she could figure out. Whether caused by her anger or her frustration or even the pain of a stubbed toe, who could say, but she was definitely getting some of her confidence back.

"I can do this," she suddenly said aloud. "Yeah, just keep telling yourself that," she added. She looked up at the cab. "No time like the present." She walked around the front of the tractor, noticing for the first time that the front-end loader had been mounted, ready for the snow that was sure to come. The bucket was lowered to the ground. As she made her way to the steps leading to the driver's seat, she had to duck under a heavy electrical cord snaking from the tractor to the workbench beside it. Something in her memory clicked, and she smiled with satisfaction. *I know what that cord is for, a heater to keep the oil in the engine warm.* Without it, she remembered her dad telling her, it's practically impossible to start a diesel engine in cold weather. *I wonder how much more he told me that I can dig out of my memory bank. It better be a lot.*

She yanked the plug, coiled the wire, and tossed it on the bench, then walked to the overhead door of the shed and punched the opener button. The grinding sound as the door slowly rose got Sugar excited again. The dog bounded out onto the drive then back in again, looking up at Katie. "You haven't heard that for a while, have you, girl?" She gave the dog a pat. "But you'd better give me plenty of room. Okay? I can't promise I can get this big thing to go where I want it to." She pulled her hood up against the cold wind and slipped her mittens back on before heading back to the side of the tractor. "Well, here goes nothing," she murmured as she wrapped her mittened right hand around the grab bar and climbed to the first step. She worked the latch on the cab door, pulled it open, and stepped on up into the cab. She dropped into the big seat and grabbed the wheel like she knew what she was doing.

She sat for a few minutes looking over the maze of gauges and levers and buttons, trying to jog her memory. *How many years has it been? I swear, I don't remember so many doodads. Looks like a spaceship. Oh, brother, have I got a lot to learn.* She depressed the clutch and worked the gearshift lever through a few of the notches, then reached for the ignition key and turned it hard. The engine ground noisily for a few seconds and then roared to life.

She grinned like a two-year-old riding a rocking horse and sat enjoying the deep throbbing for a moment or two before she edged the throttle forward, bringing the pitch of the engine a step higher. She could feel the power pulsing through her hands as they held the wheel. She jerked the gear lever into reverse and looked behind her for the dog, who had wisely found refuge by the front-porch steps. The porch door opened slowly, and Gram's head and shoulders appeared around it. Katie couldn't see from the tractor seat, but she just knew Gram's face was a picture of concern. *Oh, great, just what I need, an audience.* She took her foot off the clutch quickly, and the big tractor bucked jerkily backward. She jammed her foot down hard on the clutch and hesitated for a moment before trying again. This time she eased her foot back more slowly, and the tractor moved smoothly out of the shed.

She turned the wheel sharply to maneuver the tractor for a straight shot at the wide-open space between the machine shed and the barn. She had already decided that would be her practice field. She heard an unpleasant scraping noise and slammed her foot on the clutch again. "What on earth is that?" she said out loud. Looking out the windshield, she could see a path where the loader bucket, stretched on the ground in front of the tractor, had gouged through the soft dirt of the machine shed and then the packed rock driveway outside. "Whoops," she said softly.

Gingerly she tried a likely lever, and the bucket lifted slowly off the ground. "Yes!" she shouted, clenching one mittened fist in front of her. She slipped the gear lever into first gear and eased off the clutch again. The tractor moved smoothly forward toward her practice field. She grinned. Just like riding a bicycle. You never forget. Only then did she see the dark blue pickup stopped on the road. It began to accelerate slowly almost the moment she noticed it. Katie could see David's grinning face. Or was she imagining it? She couldn't be sure. She groaned. How long has he been watching? "I'll show you," she said aloud. "You just wait. I'll show you."

David put his foot down hard on the accelerator, embarrassed that he'd been seen. Otis chuckled to himself. He was getting used to a wild ride whenever these two were in sight of each other. "She seems to be gettin' the hang of it," he drawled.

"Driving around the yard is one thing. Planting a straight row of corn is another altogether," David said grimly, eyes straight ahead.

Otis glanced over at him. "Ya don't think she kin do it?"

"Let's just say I've got my doubts. You can't learn how to farm overnight. No way." Suddenly his voice sounded far away, as if he were talking to himself. "She's going to need help, but she's just too blasted stubborn to ask for it. And I'd help if she asked, but I'm sure not going with my hat in my hand to offer." He jerked his head suddenly toward Otis as if he had forgotten his hired man was there.

"You keep that under that big hat of yours, you understand?"

Otis looked straight ahead. "Whatever you say, boss."

"And stop with that boss stuff. Nobody goes around calling somebody else boss. At least not around here."

Otis nodded, but he couldn't keep another toothy grin from covering his face. He was getting a kick out of watching these two. And along with that, he was just downright happy. Finally he was beginning to make some sense out of his life. He had to pinch himself to make sure it wasn't all a dream. He felt like some big, old lop-eared hound dog who'd just been invited to Thanksgiving dinner. A big part of it was because he was leaving in less than an hour for Des Moines to pick up Becky and the baby. That was, for sure, enough, but it wasn't all. He thanked his lucky stars he'd landed feetfirst right in the middle of a whole herd of nice folks. He still got chicken flesh up the back of his neck when he thought about the fine house he'd soon be showing off to Becky. And thanks to Grandma Pitcher and a crowd of folks he'd never laid eyes on before, it was loaded to the rafters with more stuff than you could ever dream of if you lived to be a hundred.

And then there was this boss who didn't want to be a boss. Otis had learned right off that what you see is what you get with this fellow. A straight shooter if he'd ever seen one. Oh, sure, he was a little uptight. Well, maybe more than a little uptight. But nobody's perfect. And Otis knew full well what his problem was anyway. Dave Cairn had sworn off women for too long. And Otis knew for a fact that wasn't good for any man. It was as plain as the nose on your face to see. He'd been burned once, and now he was staying away from the fire. Otis was sure that wasn't the way things were supposed to work. Adam had his Eve, and every man needed his filly by his side. That's the way he figured it anyway. And just as sure as he knew his name was Otis Skibby, he knew there was something going on between those two or, more like it, something that was wanting to go on if they'd just let it. But he'd never seen such a stubborn pair. *They make any mule I've ever knowed look downright agreeable,* he thought to himself with another smile.

Heavy snow fell the next day. Otis made it back from Des Moines with Becky and the baby just before the first big flakes started swirling from the sky. It was good to have someplace to call their own, especially on such a night, when the wind grew to a howl and the snow flailed against the north windows. Becky settled the baby in her crib and wandered from room to room touching each piece of furniture, a look of awe on her face. Otis followed her proudly. "You got to meet these folks, hon. They're as friendly as cows at feedin' time. I swear I don't know where half this stuff come from. It just appeared like out a the heavens." Becky smiled up at him and slipped her arm around his lean waist.

Katie carried her second cup of breakfast coffee to the living room window and peered out. She could just make out the dark shape of the machine shed, but that was about all. A drift at least four feet high ran from the tree just outside the front door of the house to the middle of the yard. And the snow was still coming, sideways, driven by a wind that was gusting to fifty miles an hour if you could believe the announcer on KPTI.

Katie went back to the kitchen, where Gram was clearing the table. "I'll bet the kids around here are loving this. No school. And by the looks of it, there won't be any for a couple of days at least."

Gram smiled. "I'll bet the kids aren't the only ones who like those snow days."

"You've got that right. Trouble with this storm is, it's too soon after Christmas vacation. The kids and teachers aren't sick of each other yet.'' She rinsed her cup in the sink. ''Looks like I'm going to get to try out that snow scoop on the tractor.''

Gram put her hands on her hips. ''You're not going out with it blizzarding like this!''

''I know, I know. Settle down, Gram. I'm not that crazy. I'd be wasting my time anyway when it's snowing like it is. No, today I start my crash course. 'Everything You Wanted To Know About Farming in Two Months.' '' She looked at her grandmother and couldn't keep panic from showing. ''Can you believe it, Gram? I've got to be out in the field in just a little more than two months.''

''I still wish you'd talk to David. He'd be happy to help. I just know it.''

''Gram, we've been down this road before. I'm not going to give that man the satisfaction. So let's just drop it. You didn't see him laughing yesterday while I was trying to drive the tractor the first time.''

''Katie, I can't believe he'd laugh at you like that. It just doesn't seem like him.''

''Well, I saw him and that's what he was doing. So believe it.'' She marched angrily into her father's office, slumped into the chair, and began to sort noisily through the material she intended to study. Trouble was, she wasn't sure herself she'd seen David Cairn laughing at her. She thought she had, but maybe she was just imagining things. Or maybe it was Otis. Or maybe . . . oh, she didn't know. And why was David looking at her like that the other day? She saw those eyes again studying her, and a slight smile replaced her frown. The tension in her face eased, and she stared dreamily into space. Suddenly her eyes snapped back into clear focus on the desk in front of her. Now, stop that, she said to herself, and pulled the stack of reading material toward her.

She read and took notes most of the day. She found old copies of past seed and fertilizer orders and learned where her dad did business. She studied the farm map for acreages and computed how much she would need of everything. She spent hours skimming through her dad's magazines and stopped to read any article that promised a how-to explanation. She had a problem. These articles were like graduate school stuff to her. They assumed at least a basic understanding. What she needed was something simpler. She wondered if there was such a thing. A book on farming for someone who's never farmed. There must be such a thing, she thought, and decided to try the town library when the weather improved.

Gram came in to say she had called Otis, but he was out working with the cattle. "Can you imagine going out in weather like this?" she asked. Anyway, she had talked to Becky and found out they had made it back safe and sound from Des Moines before the snow even started. "She's a sweet person," Gram added. Katie smiled up at her grandmother from the swivel chair. One phone call and the two were fast friends already. Why did that not surprise her? Gram had promised a visit just as soon as the weather cleared. "I can't wait to get my hands on that baby," she said.

The phone rang in the middle of the afternoon, and Gram answered. Katie could hear her voice from the living room but couldn't make out what she was saying. She came into the office a few minutes later. "That was David. He sounded awful. They're having a time of it with the cattle in this weather. He just called to be sure we were all right. Wasn't that nice of him?" Katie nodded and smiled. It was true. There still was a friendliness among neighbors here that she certainly missed in the city.

She didn't even try to dig out for another day. When she finally did go out on Wednesday morning, the wind had died, it was sunny and bright, and the air was bitingly cold. The county snowplow had made a pass down their road about nine o'clock, throwing a cloud of snow into the ditch.

They were running low on a few things and needed to make a trip into town, but not before she cleared the yard, that was for sure. The pickup was a four-wheel drive, but that didn't mean it could climb over six-foot snowdrifts.

She surveyed the white wasteland outside the front door and decided it was definitely beautiful if all you had to do was look at it. Sugar joined her, leaping from one drift to another. She had invited the spaniel onto the porch at the first threat of the storm, and it was a good thing, too. The doghouse door was completely blown full of snow. She was grateful there were no cattle to worry about, but she felt sorry for those neighbors, including David and Otis, who had that battle on their hands. She marveled at the strange patterns of the drifts. One monstrous one ran from the shelter of the machine shed to a cluster of trees some thirty feet away. It looked like a giant white wave frozen in motion. A delicate edge seemed to defy gravity, jutting at least a foot beyond the face of the drift, and the whole thing feathered into a gentle curve around one of the trees.

Katie had the tractor started in no time and backed carefully out of the shed. It took her a little practice to catch on to operating the bucket. Several times she grabbed the wrong lever and dumped a whole load of snow when she really meant to lift it off the ground, but she caught on soon enough. And in less than an hour she had the drive and the area around the garage clear, with a huge pile of the white stuff on the far side of the machine shed to show for her efforts. She even felt confident enough to flick on the radio, and the music that filled the glassed-in cab made the job seem almost easy. She was getting the hang of it now. She eased the big tractor back into the shed feeling positively exhilarated. She cut the engine and climbed down out of the cab. She plugged the heater back in and made her way around the front of the tractor. She had just punched the button for the overhead door when she saw

David's pickup turn into the drive as the big door rattled noisily down.

She stepped outside as the door dropped shut behind her. David pulled to a stop beside her and opened the window. Katie was shocked to see how tired he looked. He had at least a day's growth of beard, and his face was haggard, his eyes red and puffy.

"What happened to you? You look awful."

He smiled weakly. "Thanks a lot. I needed that." He rubbed his eyes with the back of his hand. "Haven't had too much sleep the last couple of nights." His voice was dull and lifeless. "We've had a devil of a time with the cattle. Especially at the north place, where Otis is. Had a hard time getting hay to them, and then last night the tank heater went out, and we had to do something with that before the water froze up. About half a dozen head got caught at the far end of the pasture at the start of the storm. We couldn't get to them, and I don't suppose we could have done much with them if we had." He sighed. "They didn't make it."

Katie remembered with a twinge of guilt that there was more to a blizzard than vacation from school. She knew what the loss of six head of cattle could do to a farmer's profit margin. "I'm sorry," she said. "Come on in. You look like you could use a cup of coffee."

David smiled up at her from the cab, and their eyes met. "Thanks, that sounds tempting, but I'd better not. I had to stay at Otis's last night because their road blew shut. The plow just went by up there, and I'm on my way home to see if the rest of the herd made it through the night. Just stopped by to make sure everything was okay here."

Katie suddenly remembered her earlier ugly scene when David was just showing this very same concern for her grandmother, and she felt guilty all over again. "That's very nice of you. Thanks, thanks a lot."

He slipped the truck into gear. "Nice job on the snow," he said.

Katie beamed at the unexpected praise as she looked about proudly at the yard scraped clean of snow. She hoped he didn't notice the few dark spots where the bucket had gouged through the crushed rock and taken a bite out of the dirt below. "Why, thank you. I did catch on to it pretty well." When she glanced back at him, she saw that just the hint of a smile was starting.

"I sure hope you have plenty of fuel in your tractor," he said as the smile, now positively gleeful, spread across his face. "'Cause you're not going to get to that tank for a while." Katie turned in the direction he was nodding and heard him chuckle as he backed the truck away for a straight shot out the driveway. Sure enough, there was the 500-gallon diesel fuel tank neatly barricaded by all the snow she had scraped from the yard. He was right, of course. If she needed a fill, it was either move the snow again, only this time very, very carefully, or wait for a thaw. And naturally, he *would* have to notice. Katie stamped her foot. "Oh, that man!" she shouted through gritted teeth as the pickup swung out onto the road.

Chapter Seven

The weather did an about-face over the next several days, fooling, at least for the time being, the local old-timers who were predicting the winter of the decade. In fact, the temperature made it nearly to sixty by the next Sunday, and Katie had the last laugh. The pile of snow around the fuel tank had all but disappeared a week after the storm.

She and Gram visited Otis and Becky, and they found the couple hadn't come down from their cloud in spite of the bad days and nights Otis had put in with the cattle. Katie liked Becky from the start. Mrs. Becky Skibby, as Otis was so proud to introduce her, had a plain but certainly not unattractive face. Her complexion was fair, almost ghostlike, and her rejection of even the hint of makeup didn't help matters. Her hair, dark, long, and straight, hung below her shoulders.

She seemed shy when Katie and Gram settled around the kitchen table, but opened up and even became talkative after a while. Who wouldn't come out of her shell with Gram around? Katie noticed how interested Becky was in everything. Instead of being bored by the long bus ride from Oklahoma, she was still excited by what she'd seen out the window along the way. Katie soon found out why. Becky had never been more than thirty miles from home in her life until then. Katie guessed the homesickness would set in when the novelty of the move faded. She didn't learn until later, when the two became good friends, that there really wasn't much home left in Oklahoma to be sick about. Her mother had died when Becky was thirteen, and her father, never much of a father to her, had remarried three years later. His new wife made Becky feel she wasn't wanted in her own home, and she was only too happy to set up a small apartment in the basement, becoming more like a tenant than a member of the family.

She and Otis met when he was taking therapy for his bullfighting injury. She was working as a nurse's aide in the local hospital at the time. And already she was asking about the hospital in Willow Grove. Katie guessed that Gram would be volunteering for baby-sitting duty before many months went by. And when Otis came out of the nursery with little Lena Marie, fresh from her nap, Katie knew it was a done deal. The little sprite, just thirteen months old that very day, peeked shyly from the safety of Otis's shoulder at the two strangers, but smiled broadly when Katie made a face at her. Before long, she was making toddling steps from between Otis's knees to first Grandma and then Katie, but when they moved to pick her up, she giggled happily and escaped back to her father. She had totally captivated them, and she knew it.

"I don't know if that's such a good idea. You saw how shy Becky is, and Otis isn't much better." The two were on their way home, and Gram had just unveiled her latest inspiration, a neighborhood surprise party to welcome the Skibbys to Willow Grove.

"Nonsense. It'll be good for them. Give 'em a chance to meet everyone."

"But is that kind of thing done anymore? People nowadays like to keep to themselves more than they did . . ." she hesitated, searching for the least dangerous path, ". . . you know, some years ago."

Her grandmother shot her a look. "You mean back in the dark ages, when I was your age?"

"I didn't say that."

"No, but you were thinking it." Katie knew she had opened a can of worms. "The trouble with young folks today is they want to do everything themselves. Don't want to get involved. Don't want to even know who lives right next door to them. Why one person I know wouldn't even ask her nice neighbor for help even if her life depended on it."

Now it was Katie's turn to glare. "You won't give up on that, will you?" She turned into their lane. "Okay, if you must go through with this little party, at least warn the two of them. It's not fair to spring it on them. They may hide in the basement and not come out."

"Better to keep it a surprise," Gram insisted. "That way they won't have a chance to worry about it."

The surprise part of the plan gnawed at Katie for the next several days, and the day before the big affair, she finally came to a decision. Her grandmother was in high gear. Between phone calls with her fellow conspirators (oh, no, she hadn't hatched this little plan all by herself) and baking and who knows what else, the kitchen looked like a battle zone. Katie was doing her share. After all, she liked a party as much as anyone, but still there was a worry. It just didn't seem right not to tell someone that twenty guests were about to drop in announced. She got her orders for another trip to town, the third in the last two days, this time for five pounds of flour, a small ham, and a pint of sour cream.

She headed straight for the pickup. But she opted for the scenic route to Willow Grove, a route that just happened to take her past the Skibby bungalow. And while she was in the neighborhood, why not stop in for a visit? Wasn't Gram herself preaching friendliness to neighbors? And once inside, settled at the kitchen table over a hot cup of coffee, who could blame her for accidentally letting the surprise party out of the bag? She watched the pair closely as they exchanged surprised glances. Otis actually rocked his chair back on two legs and let out a quiet, "Well, I'll be." She worried that maybe she hadn't thought this thing through completely. What would she do if they took off for parts unknown? But she had misjudged them and, of course, her grandmother. She was finally coming to the conclusion that everything that woman planned was just the right thing to do. "It's because her heart's in the right place," her father would have said. They were actually pleased, both of them. *Touched* might be a better word for it. Oh, sure, they were shocked. And even a little embarrassed at "all the fuss" as Otis called it.

Becky summed it up in her cute drawl, "The people here have been so sweet. I've never seen the like. We were just wondering how we could thank everyone for the furniture. Weren't we, Otis?"

"Right y'are, darlin'," he said turning toward her.

"Now you can do it in person tomorrow night," she said, patting him on the shoulder.

Otis jumped in his chair and splashed his coffee onto the table. He sprang to the sink for the dishcloth. "Now wait just a minute here. How did I get volunteered for such a chore as talkin' in front of a crowd a folks?"

Becky touched his hand as he corralled the spill with the cloth. "Sweetie, any man who can stand up to a cantankerous old bull doesn't need to worry about saying thank you to a few friends." She smiled, and it was a done deal. Katie wondered who the real bullfighter in this household was.

It was obvious that no one had ever cared enough about these two to do something like this before. And as for Katie's worry about a crowd of guests descending unannounced, probably based on her own shortcomings as a housekeeper, she could see at a glance that Becky was one of those neataholics who never had to give the slightest thought to being caught with a messy house.

As Katie pulled on her coat to leave, a new worry struck her. Gram would know who spilled the beans if these two didn't act surprised. "Listen, Gram will kill me with a slow poison in my breakfast cereal if she finds out I told you about this."

"Don't you worry none about that," said Otis. "We'll act as surprised as a milk cow in a barn full of icicle salesmen. Right, hon?"

Becky wrinkled her nose at him. "I guess so. Not that I know what that means. Don't worry," she said quietly to Katie, "we'll never let on we knew anything about it."

The Cairn place was the staging area for the big party. The plan was to meet at five o'clock and move on to the scene of the party for dinner or, as everyone in these parts called it, supper. Mrs. Pitcher had begged a ride from David for her and Katie, "to avoid parking problems," as she explained to Katie. He made the short trip down the road early, about four-thirty, driving his silver Buick Park Avenue to accommodate the three comfortably. He began to wonder if he should have taken his pickup when they started to load in the goodies Mrs. Pitcher and Katie had created. There were casserole dishes and boxes of sandwiches and covered pans of brownies and Tupperware barrels of cookies. They hurried back to his place before the rest of the armada arrived and waited inside in his spacious kitchen. Katie didn't think she had ever been in the Cairn house before. Maybe once with her father a long time ago, but she couldn't remember. Her grandmother was occupying David with some detail about the party, so she took the opportunity to look around as unobtrusively as possible. She couldn't help herself. She was curious.

From where she sat at the kitchen table, she could see

into the living room, where a soft light was burning. She could just make out a stone fireplace with a large painting over the mantle and an arrangement of comfortable-looking chairs in muted shades. She wondered if the house was done to his taste or that of his divorced wife. *He probably hasn't changed a thing since she left,* Katie thought. Her eyes scanned the kitchen floor and the spotless counter and shining sink. *Does he have a cleaning service, or is he a neatness freak like Becky?* She suddenly became aware of the silence. She glanced up quickly. Both David and her grandmother were staring at her. Had someone asked her a question? Katie smiled. "Did you say something?"

"I wondered if you wanted to see my new living room. I just had the furniture delivered yesterday."

Katie looked through the door. "Oh, there's the living room. I hadn't noticed." Her face flushed at the lie. He must have seen her gawking. She sprang from her chair and stuck her head through the door to look around. Yes, the room was beautifully decorated in Early American. Suddenly, she was aware that he was standing beside her. She could smell his aftershave, and the sleeve of his cardigan lightly brushed her shoulder as he slipped by to turn on another light.

"My ex-wife insisted on some awful modern stuff. We had it everywhere, and none of it was comfortable. I should have gotten rid of it a long time ago." He had plopped into one of the wing-backs by the fireplace and stretched back. "So what do you think?" He pointed to a smaller wing-back on the other side of the fireplace. "Try that one." Katie had followed him slowly into the room. She sat in the chair, carefully at first, but couldn't resist sinking back into its luxurious comfort. He watched her. "Was I right? Isn't that a chair you could live in? Even good for naps," he added, resting his head against one of the wings and closing his eyes.

"Umm," Katie murmured as she watched him through half open eyes.

He opened his eyes and gazed contentedly at the painting above the mantle. "And I finally got great-grandma and -grandpa Cairn back up where they belong."

Katie followed his gaze to the painting she had caught a glimpse of from the kitchen. It was obviously a wedding portrait, very dark and very crudely done as far as she was concerned. The heads of the couple seemed to be too big for their bodies. She could see no family resemblance between David and either one of the wooden figures. Katie focused on the hands of the woman, gently folded in her lap. They looked more like claws than hands. *I think I'd have to throw in with the ex–Mrs. Cairn on this one,* she thought. *I hope it wasn't a marriage breaker. It would go nicely over the bed in a spare bedroom.* She glanced quickly back at David. He was still looking proudly at the painting. *Oh, please, please, please don't ask me what I think of it,* she pleaded silently. *My limit is one bad lie a day.*

Grandma Pitcher was standing in the doorway smiling as she watched the two by the fireplace. She heard a sound and glanced out the kitchen window to see two cars pull in, one right after the other, and she could see others coming up the road. "They're here," she shouted, bringing David and Katie out of their chairs.

In the hubbub that followed, Katie wished more than once that she hadn't blown the surprise part of the party. She felt like a traitor in their midst. She could only hope that Otis and Becky could act their way through it. She was afraid the tidy house would give her away. And how could she explain the truth to these neighbors? That Becky was Martha Stewart in disguise? No, they were going to suspect something; she just knew it.

She had seen most of these folks at her parents' funerals. It was good to see them again under happier circumstances, and this time to really feel a part of them. After all, she was a farmer too. She wondered how many of them knew about her plans. Knowing how rumors spread in this community, she guessed they probably all did.

They milled around, waiting for everyone to arrive. Some decided to leave their cars here and piled in with friends only after they had transferred their goodies from trunk to trunk. Katie guessed they had enough food among them to feed most of Willow Grove. When everyone was accounted for, they drove out the lane, with David in the lead. Once on the road, they formed a long line and moved slowly toward Otis and Becky's. The sun was just sinking below the horizon as they pulled into the Skibby driveway.

Otis and Becky deserved at least an Academy Award nomination for their acting job as far as Katie was concerned. She guessed it probably wasn't all acting. They were truly overwhelmed by the numbers of new friends who showed up, and they stood at the door and shook hands trying to place faces with names. Becky even had the table set for supper and had something going on the stove. She's good at this sneaky stuff, Katie thought as she helped clear the table and put in extra leaves. Otis was scurrying for more chairs, but Grandma Pitcher had thought of everything. Several guests had been assigned to bring folding chairs.

The men gravitated to the living room. A tub with iced-down beer and soda appeared on the porch, but fresh coffee was still popular. The serving table was ready in no time, but a few casseroles had to be reheated before Grandma shouted from the kitchen, "Supper's on. Come and get it while it's hot." The line moved slowly past the table. There was some friendly bantering by those waiting. "Hey, don't let old Hank up there first. Won't be nothing left for the rest of us." "I've been on a diet since Christmas, but I guess I can fall off the wagon just this once." "Hey, Otis, okay if we come back tomorrow night for leftovers?"

The diners sat on chairs hugging the walls of the living room, balancing paper plates on their knees. Baby Lena was having the time of her life toddling back and forth between the crowd in the living room and a handful of children who had been assigned an open space on the kitchen linoleum. The talk was subdued as everyone concentrated on food, but things began to liven up as the empty plates were finally set aside.

"Say, Otis, how is this here boss of yours? He been treatin' you right?" It was time for fun, Katie could tell from her place next to her grandmother. The one talking was Otto Struebler, the undisputed mouth of any gathering, be it a church social or a seed corn sales dinner. Wherever there was a crowd, you could hear his high-pitched, nasal voice above the rest. He was still farming at the ripe old age of seventy-two, and Katie took heart as she looked across at the man. A scrawnier specimen it was hard to imagine. *If he can do it, so can I,* she reasoned.

Otis shifted in his chair. "He's been right square with me. Fact is, I ain't never had a better. He's outright given us this house rent free, ya know."

Katie glanced quickly across at David. His head was bowed now, and she noticed his face had reddened.

"Oh, don't worry none about that, Otis." It was Otto Struebler again. "He'll work it out a ya when spring plantin' starts." Everyone laughed.

David raised his head. "Last week Otis wasn't so sure the move up north was the best thing he'd ever done."

"They get snow down there where you come from, don't they?" asked Ron Hemmingford, a short, paunchy fellow who had been a good friend of Katie's dad.

"Oh, sure, but it don't always come sideways." There was laughter and a lot of head-nodding.

"You lose any cattle?" asked Ron, looking across at David.

"Six head."

"I talked to a fellow over by Sheffield the other day," said Tig Sorenstam, a tall, lean fellow who looked as if he could have posed for the *American Gothic* painting. "He's got a neighbor lost fifty head." There were groans and whistles from the circle of neighbors. "That sure would put a dent in the old bottom line. Suppose the bank would write that off for ya?"

"Oh, yeah," someone said, "you could count on that."

"See what you're getting yourself into, Katie Rourke?" said Otto, eying Katie sharply, that ever-present smirk dominating his face. "You left that big-paying part-time job back there in Illinois to get yourself mixed up in all this?"

Katie looked across at him, a slight smile on her lips. So, it's my turn, she thought. "I'd gotten myself into such a high tax bracket, I had to do something to get rid of all that extra money."

"Well, you come to the right place for that," someone in the circle said. "You heard about the farmer who won the lottery? Somebody asked him what he was gonna do with the money. Said he was gonna keep farming till it was all gone." There were only a few chuckles. They'd all heard this one before.

"So you're really aiming to farm your daddy's place all by yourself?" asked Mr. Struebler, this time without the smile. He really wanted some confirmation of what he'd been hearing.

"I'm going to try," she said warily. The tone of his voice made Katie feel more of an outsider than she had since she'd been home.

"Uh-huh," he said, looking around the circle to see how the news struck everyone. "Well, now, I think that's just mighty fine," he said sarcastically. "Now if them guvment fellas come knockin' on our door askin' if we're politically correct, we can tell 'em sure, we got ourselves a girl farmer." His wife, Hilda, who towered over him but rarely said a word, now glared down at the top of his head and to the surprise of everyone blurted, "Otto!" with such force it was almost like she had said an obscene word. But it wasn't enough to stop him. In fact, it might have spurred him on, so no one would think she had the power to stop him. "So you think you can do it all by yourself without your daddy around to tell you what to do?" he added.

Before Katie could open her mouth to respond, David broke in. "Otto, why don't you mind your own business. Katie's going to do just fine." Katie stared at him in shock. She hadn't expected him to defend her, that's for sure. And she wasn't the only one who stared. These folks had tolerated Otto Struebler's harangues for too long. It was time to pile on.

"Otto, you're a great one to talk," said Gloria Hemmingford, Ron's wife. "It's the pot calling the kettle black. If the likes a you can still put in a crop, any woman here ought to be able to do it."

One of the other women spoke up. "There's nothing to driving those tractors anyway. Air-conditioning and stereo and power steering. It's almost like a car."

"Come on now, Hazel, there's a little more to it than that, and you know it," said Tig Sorenstam.

"Maybe so, Tig," said Gloria Hemmingford with a growing heat in her voice, "but you're just afraid to admit that Katie might make a go of it. Otto and some of the rest of you are still living in the dark ages. Well, it's about time you woke up. There are women doctors and lawyers and judges and mechanics and even truck drivers. So why not a woman farmer?" Several women in the circle nodded their agreement.

Ron Hemmingford turned toward his wife in surprise. "What is this all about? Are you some kind of frustrated women's libber? And I can't believe this coming from you. Why just this very morning you said that Katie must be crazy to just waltz in here and think she can start farming."

His wife turned on him, her eyes flashing. "I never said that."

"Those were your exact words."

She folded her arms and sniffed angrily. "Well, maybe I did. But so what? Maybe I've changed my mind."

"Since this morning?"

Several of the men guffawed at that.

Gloria looked angrily about her. "Why not? You got a problem with that?"

Katie was perched on her chair, hoping a black hole might swallow her up. *Are we having fun yet?* She hadn't really planned on being the center of attention at a neighborhood roast. And she certainly didn't like the idea of turning the men against the women. She was shocked at their strong feelings. She knew all along they were probably talking about her and her scheme of farming the land, though she doubted they knew her reasons. But she hadn't expected them to be choosing up sides like they were. And now the chair next to her creaked, and Katie knew her grandmother was about to wade into all this.

"If David says Katie can do it, then that's good enough for me."

Katie reached over and patted her grandmother's arm to thank her, but also to remind her she'd said enough. She raised her head then and looked around the circle. "Could we move on to something else? I don't like to see you all fighting. Anyway, this is supposed to be a party for Otis and Becky."

But it wasn't to be. Old Otto had the unfailing habit of putting a punctuation mark on any discussion. And right at this moment, he wanted the last word more than usual. He was still smarting from his wife's interference, and what Gloria Hemmingford had said hadn't helped his disposition any. Only what he was about to say next was outrageous even by his standards. "Ain't you still got some a them fancy books on farming they give out in college?" he asked, looking David square in the face. "Maybe you and Katie here could get together for some book learnin' sessions. You been needin' a little female companionship since that wife a yours up and left ya."

David sucked in a sharp breath and turned a steely glare on Otto. The two had had their problems over the years. Just why, David was never sure, but the old codger was always ready to snipe at him. No question about it, Otto had hit him where he hurt this time, his failed marriage. His feelings for his ex-wife had long ago died. That was no consideration. But the old duff was right about one thing. David hadn't been able to establish any kind of relationship with another woman, and he wasn't happy that his neighbors had been reminded of that fact. Then he thought about what Otto had said about Katie, and felt close to really losing his temper. Why should she be brought into all this? "What kind of a crack is that to make?" he snapped. "You owe Katie an apology, do you hear me?"

Katie couldn't keep out of it. "Me? You're the one who deserves the apology. Mr. Struebler, that was an ugly thing to say."

Even Otto knew he had gone too far this time. His face turned pale and his trademark smirk had left him entirely. "Simmer down, would ya? I didn't mean no harm," he stammered. "I was just kiddin' around." That wasn't exactly an apology, but everyone there knew it was about as close as Otto Struebler was likely to come to one.

An uncomfortable quiet settled over the party. Katie wasn't sure what to make of things. Could she expect the cold shoulder from these folks who had been friends of her parents? If so, she was in trouble. She needed all the help she could get. The tension finally eased when Baby Lena's squeal broke the silence as she teetered through the door from the kitchen looking for her mother. The party went on. Katie even got some words of encouragement, but from the women only. Otis managed to get through his thank-you speech. Otto and Hilda Struebler missed it, though. They went home early.

Chapter Eight

The morning after the party, Otis came out to find a thin coating of ice on the tank used to water the cattle. The heater was stone cold to his touch. This was the same heater that had failed during the blizzard. He had been nursing it along for the past week, but the flame just wouldn't burn right, and kept going out in the least bit of wind. David pulled in as Otis was breaking the layer of ice out of the tank. He climbed out of the truck. "Mornin', Otis. It's up to its old tricks again, I see." Otis returned the greeting and nodded.

David pulled the cover off the burner and peered inside. He straightened up, his hands on his hips. "We can't keep playing around with this thing. If it gets really cold again, the tank will freeze solid."

"I expect some a them burner holes must be rusted shut," Otis suggested.

"Looks like it. I'm going to run to town for a new burner. Can you take care of the hay by yourself?" Otis nodded. "Oh, and if I'm not back by the time you're done, see if you can get that old burner out. Be sure to turn off the gas at the tank." He climbed back into the truck and backed the fifty yards or so to the turnaround by the garage.

When David got back, Otis had almost finished with the old burner. He pulled it free and the two inspected it. They had the new one in place in no time, but it took a few minutes to complete the gas connection. David stood and dug in his coat pocket for a match. Otis was sitting on an overturned pail. He had already put the tools back in the big metal toolbox.

"So you and Becky survived the party all right?"

"Oh, sure. Right nice of everyone to come."

David had come up empty in his search for a match. "You got a match?" he asked. Otis patted his jacket pocket and produced a small box of stick matches. David lit one and cupped it in his hand to protect it from what little wind there was, then held it over the pilot until the blue flame appeared. "Sorry about the little scene last night. Folks usually get along a little better than that." He stood and adjusted the thermostat until the burner came on.

"Weren't no harm done," Otis said. "That there Otto fellow seemed to have it in for you a mite."

David looked at Otis and raised his eyebrows. "I noticed." He pulled his stocking cap down to cover his ears. "Oh, he's not a bad old coot. Problem is he just never shuts his mouth. He's got something stuck in his craw about going to school to learn to farm. He thinks it all has to be handed down from father to son. Too bad he and Hilda never had any kids, so he's got no one to pass it on to." He turned the thermostat until the burner went out, then raised it until the blue flame ignited once again. "He was probably spouting off about that long before I ever went to Iowa State, but he keeps hammering me about it every chance he gets. But I couldn't believe the way he lit into Katie. You'd almost think he didn't want her to make a go of it." He leaned down and eyed the burner. "Doesn't sound like he's alone, either."

Otis was scratching in the dirt with a stick. "Almost sounds like another feller I know when he got wind a what she was up to," he said innocently.

David straightened up. "You're not talking about *me*?"

"Could be."

"Is that really the way I've been sounding?"

"Could be."

He nodded, thinking of a few choice scenes. "Yeah, I suppose you're right. I have been a horse's ass." He stared down into the water in the tank. "I tell you that woman is something else. She sure is the exact opposite of Joan."

Otis had pushed it this far. He decided he might as well go the whole way. "You know she's partial toward ya," he said simply.

David turned toward him in surprise. "What's that?"

"She's got a hankerin' for ya."

"But you just said not more than two minutes ago that she thinks I'm a horse's ass."

"I never said no such a thing," Otis protested. "You said that your own self."

"Well, you didn't disagree," David said gruffly. "Anyway, that's probably what she *has* been thinking after some of the stupid stuff I've said. And now you come along and say she's got a hankering for me."

"Yup. It's a fact, too."

"And how did you come up with this fact, as you call it?"

"It's about as plain as the nose on your face."

David put the metal cover over the burner. His voice was composed. "So, I'm waiting. How did you arrive at this little discovery?"

"Well." Otis hesitated. "Me and Becky was talkin' about it last night."

"So Becky's in on this too, huh?"

Otis was beginning to wish he'd kept his mouth shut. He closed up the toolbox. But he had gone this far, so he decided to blunder on. "We both come up with it together. It's kinda like she's all moony-eyed when she's lookin' at ya."

David stood and zipped his coat. He dug in his pockets for his gloves, all the while watching Otis, waiting for more, but the cowboy was quiet. "You mean that's it?

That's what this is all about?'' A fit of laughter convulsed him. ''Otis, you're something else. Let's see if I've got this straight now. Either Katie's crazy about me, or she has an eye condition. Is that about right?'' He headed for the pickup, chuckling as he went. If Otis hadn't been so busy feeling sorry for himself for bringing the whole business up in the first place, he might have noticed an echo of hollowness in the laughter. Because before David even reached the truck, he was already wildly searching his memory for any hint of the look Otis and Becky claimed to have seen, and making plans for what he could do to find out if they just might be right.

The next several weeks flew by. At least to Katie they did. She was working overtime, cramming her head with as much information as possible. She knew there was little time left before she would have to take to the field with what she'd learned. She couldn't ever remember studying this hard, even in college. She read everything of her father's she could lay her hands on, even down to the manuals that had come with the new pieces of machinery. Her mother had never approved of her dad's pack rat habits, but Katie was eternally grateful that he had never thrown anything away.

She knew the features of the newest tractor as well as any salesman. And the same was true of the combine and the planter and the cultivator and you name it. Many a night she dropped off to sleep in bed only to wake groggily two hours later, the light from her lamp shining bright in her face and articles on herbicide application or soil conditioning or planting depth strewn over her bed. She was making progress, but there was so much to learn. She even berated herself at times for not paying more attention while she was living at home, forgetting she had been busy then just being a kid.

She took advantage of the stretch of good weather to

practice with some of the machinery. She hitched the disk to the tractor, connecting the hydraulic hoses and all, and even tried maneuvering this wide, unwieldy load around the yard. She raised and lowered it several times, getting the knack of the hydraulic control lever. She was careful not to go deep with the sharp disks, though, knowing they would tear up her practice area. She even started the giant combine and backed it slowly out of the machine shed. She knew she wouldn't need this hulk until harvest season many months away, but she really needed to move it to get at the planter, which she spent a good hour and a half investigating, the operator's manual clutched in one hand. Sugar watched all these strange goings-on from a distance.

She stopped by the elevator on the edge of town to order fertilizer and seed corn. To her surprise, Jake Toomes was still running the place. In fact, if she didn't know better she would swear he was decked out in the very same flannel shirt, faded blue jeans, and bright gold Dekalb hat he'd been wearing the last time she'd been inside the cluttered office. How long ago had that been? At least fifteen years, she guessed. And he couldn't have been more friendly to her. But she knew it was out of deference to her dad, a longtime customer. Of course old Jake remembered when her head barely reached the level of the counter and when she used to beg a nickel from her dad to feed the peanut machine. She had loved coming here, that's for sure, and as she looked around, much was the same. But still she felt awkward and out of place.

There were four other farmers inside, two slouched against the counter and the other two relaxing on broken-down folding chairs. This office had always been a popular gathering spot. They too were friendly, nodding as she came in, but their conversation died out as she recited her order from the sheet she'd taken from her jacket pocket. They were listening, that's for sure. And there it was. She was certain of it. An exchange of knowing smiles. Even

Jake was in on it. It was the same smile that crept onto the face of the librarian just last week when she noticed the title of the book Katie was checking out—*The Growing Season Step-by-Step.* Either she was getting paranoid, or the whole town was in on her change-of-career plans. She always believed news traveled fast around here, but this was ridiculous. Katie decided she would take Otto Struebler over the silent smirkers any day. At least he was honest. He thought she was crazy for trying such a harebrained scheme, and he didn't mind saying it.

And as if she didn't have enough to worry about, cramming a lifetime of farming savvy into three months and trying to interpret hidden meaning in the smiles of everyone from the grocery clerk to the usher at church, her personal life was in a shambles. Steve, back in Rockford, was becoming a problem. He was nice enough, but not someone she wanted to get serious with. She thought of him as a friend and that's all. She tried to say as much in a letter soon after settling in at home. She could have called, but a letter seemed a better way to keep him at arm's length. She thought she had spelled everything out clearly in her letter. In fact, she really thought all had been taken care of before she left Rockford. Apparently, Steve didn't share her opinion, and he had no intention of operating under any letter-writing constraint. He called.

They talked for more than an hour. She carefully explained her plans. His reaction made Otto Struebler seem a pillar of understanding by comparison. He tried to shame her out of her plans, reminded her about duty toward profession, students, colleagues, school. She had already been down this road on her own, and she was growing definitely tired of the conversation. He suggested he would come for a visit ''to talk some sense into her head,'' as he put it. This was just too much. He was making more of their relationship than she ever thought was there. She told him so quite bluntly, she thought, and hung up.

But Steve wasn't to be so easily dissuaded. He turned to the U.S. mail to continue his appeal. Two flowery cards arrived the first week of February. Another followed the next Monday. Katie weighed a response. Deciding she had said all that needed to be said during their marathon phone conversation, she decided to ignore these latest entreaties. Another card came on Wednesday. Thrown into a foul mood the second she recognized the handwriting on the envelope, she did something she would soon regret. She tore up the card unopened.

Then there was David. Her grandmother wasn't about to let her forget about him even if she wanted to, which she didn't. Gram had blown David's defense of her at the party into practically mythical status. Katie couldn't keep thoughts of him from creeping into her daily routine, not that that was all bad. Of course, it was hard to forget about him anyway, because he kept stopping by. At least every other day, to check up on Gram, he always made a point to say. But Katie wondered if that was all there was to it. She caught him more than once studying her with a quizzical look on his face. Why just yesterday he missed his mouth and sloshed hot coffee off his chin and down his shirt, and she was positive it was because he was trying to watch her across the room while he was talking to Gram and drinking coffee all at the same time. He had grabbed his coat and bolted out the door. Katie smiled and shook her head. Could Gram be right after all? She didn't have long to wait to find out.

Chapter Nine

It was Thursday. Katie had just come back from town to pick up a prescription for her grandmother. She hung up her coat and ducked into the living room. Gram looked up from her stitching. "Did you see what's on the kitchen table?" She got to her feet and led the way to the kitchen, where a long blue box rested on the table. "It was just delivered before you got home. You must have met the delivery truck on the road. Flowers, from Orchard Florists. Must be roses. The envelope is addressed to both of us, so I waited for you. Very formal," she said as she held the envelope. " 'Mrs. Pitcher and Ms. Rourke.' Who in the world could be sending us flowers?"

"I have no idea. You open the box, and I'll open the card."

Grandma carefully undid the ribbon around the box and gently tugged the lid off. "Red roses. Aren't they beautiful?" She was counting. "A dozen. Don't they smell just like spring? They must have cost a fortune. They always raise the prices of flowers around Valentine's Day. It's a crime. Well, hurry and open the card. Let's see who they're from."

Katie slit the envelope with a long fingernail and slipped out the card, looking first for the name. "They're from David. What on earth for?" The message was handwritten in a bold, firm hand. She read it aloud. " 'I've been remiss in not thanking you two for your help on the house. Please join me for dinner tomorrow evening. I'll pick you up at six-thirty. It's signed David C." She held the card lightly and stared off into space, a hint of a smile playing at her lips.

"Now wasn't that nice of him? As if he had to go to all that trouble and expense. Don't you think that was nice? . . . Katie?"

The dreamy look left Katie's face, and she jerked her head toward her grandmother. "What? Oh, yes, that was nice."

Gram was searching in the corner cupboard for a vase, but she stopped and turned to look at her granddaughter. "Hmm, flowers and a dinner invitation."

"Now don't be getting any ideas. Your name is on the envelope too."

"I know, dear, but remember, it is the day before Valentine's Day."

"It's also Friday the thirteenth," Katie reminded her with a teasing smile.

At about five the next afternoon, Katie came into the living room from the office where she'd been working. She looked at her grandmother, who was intent on her counted cross-stitch. "We'd better be getting ready. David's coming at six-thirty, remember? I'm going to take my shower now."

Her grandmother stretched her head from side to side and massaged her neck with one hand. "Dear, I think I'm going to have to back out. I've got a terrible headache that starts here in my neck and works all the way up to my forehead. You two can go along without me. I'll just fix a sandwich for myself."

Katie smiled. "Oh no you don't. You've been working two hours on that cross-stitching, and I know you don't do that when you have a headache." She sat on the edge of a chair. "Would you please give up on the matchmaking bit? He's just being nice to us because of the work we did on the house, and I know he's trying to make up for the trouble at the party even though he doesn't have to.''

Mrs. Pitcher ran her needle through the pattern horizontally and set the round wooden frame on the table by her chair. ''But you do like him, don't you?''

''Gram, you won't give up, will you? I haven't really given it much thought,'' she lied. ''Okay, he's good-looking, I'll give you that.'' She slapped herself on the forehead. ''I can't believe I'm having this conversation with my grandmother.'' Their eyes met. ''All right, all right, he seems very nice. Are you satisfied? A bit of a chauvinist, but nice.''

Gram clicked her tongue. ''You young women and your chauvinist business. Let a man be a man, for heaven's sake. Anyway, would a chauvinist let a woman boss him around like that first wife of his did? You listen to me. He was just too sensitive for the likes of her. Show me a woman who can really appreciate a sensitive man like David, and I'll show you a marriage that will last.''

Katie pushed herself up with her hands. ''You are really getting carried away. I've got to get ready.'' She held her hand out for her grandmother. ''You're coming too. Don't even think of trying to get out of it. He invited both of us for dinner.''

Gram held out her hand and allowed herself to be pulled out of the chair. ''He likes you, you know.''

Katie was halfway to the hall, on the way to her room, but she turned. ''What makes you say that?''

''Oh, I can tell,'' her grandmother said, with a smug look on her face.

''Just how can you tell, may I ask?''

''I can tell by the way he looks at you.''

''Get out!'' she responded, but she couldn't help recalling the times she had caught him staring at her.

''Say what you will, but I can tell.''

Katie waved her hand at her grandmother and laughed. "Oh, that's right, I forgot, you're in the CIA."

Gram made a little hop as if to catch her granddaughter, but Katie danced away, giggling. "You're lucky I'm not fifteen years younger, Miss Smarty, or I'd tan your hide," she said, trying to appear solemn; but a grin gave her away.

The two were waiting at the front door when David pulled into the driveway and brought his car to a stop under the glare of the garage light. Katie left the light burning to illuminate their way coming and going. Her grandmother hurried down the steps and along the sidewalk and stood by the rear door even before David could get around the car to hold the doors for them. She's at it again, Katie thought to herself.

As David reached for the door handle, Grandma Pitcher touched his sleeve. "Those flowers were so nice."

"Yes," Katie echoed from behind. "Roses in the dead of winter!"

"I'm glad you liked them," he said as he pulled both doors open.

"But I have a bone to pick with you," said Grandma Pitcher before she got into the car.

"What's that?" he asked.

"We were just wondering why you thought you had to get those lovely flowers and take us out to supper just for being neighborly." She looked over her shoulder at Katie before she climbed into the backseat. "Weren't we, Katie?"

"Absolutely," Katie answered.

He laughed and looked in the car at them before he closed the doors. "I guess you caught me. I was just trying to figure out how to take two lovely ladies to dinner."

Katie watched him as he crossed in front of the car in full view of the headlights and the bright overhead garage light. He was wearing a dark blazer, crisply tailored, and light trousers. He had on a long-sleeved white shirt with a muted patterned tie. She was glad now she had worn her favorite red dress with the high neckline and the deeply plunging back. She had tried on three complete outfits and surveyed herself in the full-length mirror before deciding on the red. *I'm going to look idiotic,* she thought, *if we end up at Ted's Diner. I guess I can keep my coat on all evening.* Now she sighed with satisfaction at her decision. *I wonder where we are going.*

He slid behind the wheel and maneuvered the big car out of the yard and onto the gravel road. "Can you believe this day?" he asked, taking them both in with a slight turn of the head. "Look," he said, lifting both arms, "no topcoat."

"I think I heard on the radio that it got to fifty-eight," Katie said. "That just about takes care of the rest of the snow. And by the way, I can get to my gas barrel."

He laughed. "Hey, I was only kidding." He took his eyes off the road to look at her. "We're probably not done with winter yet. Anyway, you're not supposed to be too happy with the weather. Farmers are never happy with the weather. That's got to be engraved in stone somewhere. Either there's too much rain or not enough, or the rain came one week too late, or it's too hot or not hot enough, or the rain came too fast or too slow." He glanced at Katie and saw that she was smiling. She was remembering her own father's endless complaints about this very thing. She knew he used to do it on purpose, because it seemed to aggravate her mother. "That's the beauty of it," he went on. "The possibilities for dissatisfaction are practically limitless."

She laughed. "Now come on. What about today? No one could complain about this kind of weather, could they?"

"You couldn't be more wrong," he said. "If a good farmer puts his mind to it, or her mind to it," he added nodding in her direction, "there's always something about the weather to be unhappy with. Let's see." He tapped the steering wheel. "We need some snow cover for the pasture.

That's not bad for just off the top of my head. Wait a minute, wait a minute, I know I can do better." He stared at the road ahead, thinking. "Okay, I've got one. The warm weather will let the weeds sprout early." He looked over at her. "That's kind of lame, but it's the best I've got."

"You've got to be able to work in something about subsoil moisture. Dad was always complaining about subsoil moisture."

"Subsoil moisture! Very good. That's perfect, because you can use it over and over. Like, even in a heavy downpour you can always say the water is running off so fast it's not replacing the subsoil moisture. Got it? See how you can always find something wrong? I think you're going to make it." He turned and glanced quickly into the backseat. "Are you with us back there, Mrs. P?"

"I'm fine," she called from the cavern of the backseat. "I can't hear a word you young folks are saying up there, but I'm fine."

They rode in silence, deep in their own thoughts. He turned left just outside of town onto highway 50. *Where are we going?* she wondered. *There aren't any restaurants out this way, unless somebody just built one.* Then it hit her. The golf country club. She thought again about her dress, and had to physically will herself not to grin at her foresight. As they drove through the entrance, guarded by twin stone pillars, she said, "I didn't know you played golf."

"I don't. As a matter of fact, I've never even tried it. How about you?"

"No, me neither. I've played about every other sport you can name but that."

He looked her way and smiled. "Good. If we try it, we'll be on the same level." He hurried on. "We took a social membership here because my ex-wife wanted to. I just kept it because it's a nice place to eat. In fact, about the only nice place to eat in town.'' He slipped the car into a space close to the entrance.

Katie had been to the club, as the locals called it, only three times before, as well as she could remember. Two wedding receptions when she was just a kid, maybe ten or eleven, and a college graduation party that must have been five or six years ago. She surveyed the place as they waited by the receptionist's desk. Things had changed. She let David take her coat and secretly enjoyed the effect the red dress had on him.

She glanced around, recalling her last visit. She remembered lots of golf paraphernalia—old clubs hanging over the fireplace, ornately framed prints of famous golf holes, that sort of thing. She distinctly recalled a putting green made of Astroturf oddly placed just inside the front door. It made the place look like an indoor putt-putt parlor. The new look was much more tasteful. No putting green, Katie noticed immediately. The massive fireplace was still there, of course, a blazing fire brightening the room. But gone were the decorative golf clubs and vacation prints. Original oils and watercolors hung in their places. Or they looked like originals to Katie. A large watercolor, a windmill silhouetted against a setting sun, hung over the fireplace and was especially striking. Add to all that just the right combination of rich paneling, a beamed ceiling, and subdued lighting, and the first word that came to Katie was cozy—in spite of the fact that the room was a large one.

They settled at a table near the fireplace. Katie and David each ordered a glass of wine and Gram settled for a cup of coffee. ''So, what do you think of the place?'' David asked as he looked across the table at the two of them.

''Nice,'' Katie answered. ''A lot nicer than the last time I was here.''

''They remodeled it about three years ago, I think it was. My ex-wife was on the committee that drew up the plans.''

At least she got one thing right, Katie thought to herself.

Aloud, she observed, "Very tasteful. No modern furniture though," she stated flatly.

David laughed. "Funny you should mention it. She had a pretty good fight with the committee about that. She has some kind of thing about modern furniture."

A regular little modern girl, Katie thought to herself. *Thank God she didn't get her way on that one—talk about out of place.* Their drinks came. She studied David over her wineglass as she took her first sip. He seemed flushed, probably because he was sitting by the fire, she thought. Their dinner was delicious. Katie had beef medallions marinated in a delicious wine sauce. The service was excellent, and the conversation enjoyable. Gram even surprised them with the news that she had played golf on this course the very first day it opened.

"I didn't know you and Grandpa played golf!" Katie exclaimed.

"Oh, we didn't. We'd never played before in our lives. No, I take that back. I think your grandfather had played once before."

"And you played your first game here, of all places?" Katie asked. "This is a tough course, isn't it?"

Gram laughed. "That's what we found out. I lost sixteen balls by the eighth hole and your grandfather nine, I think it was." She was suddenly struck by a fit of laughter as she remembered that day. She hadn't thought of it for years. She could still see the golfers behind them shaking their fists at the inept pair for bringing play practically to a standstill. She couldn't stop laughing, and it was contagious. Katie and David joined in, until tears were running down the faces of all three. Gram had her napkin to her face. "We'd better stop this, or they'll throw us out." The thought of management tossing out a seventy-five-year-old grandmother struck Katie and David as hilarious, and the laughter started all over again. After the three had laughed themselves out, Gram finally managed to finish her story.

"We had borrowed the clubs, and we used every ball we could find in the pockets of those big bags. So we just had to quit—wasn't anything else we could do without any more balls. And we still had four more holes to play."

A burst of laughter hit David just as he was about to take a sip of wine. "Mrs. P, there are eighteen holes on the course. You still had ten to play."

"Well, whatever. I told you I didn't know anything about golf. Anyway, that took care of golfing for us. No one asked us to join the club, for sure." She took a sip of coffee and let out a long sigh. "We used to have such fun." Suddenly she looked at Katie and David and smiled. "Now, if you'll excuse me, I have to go to the little girls' room."

When she was gone, David leaned back comfortably in his chair. "She is something else."

"Isn't she a stitch, though?" Katie didn't try to keep the note of pride out of her voice. "Do you remember my grandfather?"

"I knew who he was, but I can't say I was ever really around him much."

"Well, let me tell you, they were a pair. I used to stay at their house in town when the folks were gone, or just overnight for the fun of it. It was never a dull moment. And you saw how Gram was when we worked on the house. She hasn't slowed down much."

"Well, if she has, I'd hate to try to keep up with her when she's at full speed." He folded his napkin neatly and placed it beside his plate, then looked across at Katie. "So, how are things going with you?"

"Oh, I can't complain. I've been reading everything I can get my hands on that has anything to do with farming."

He nodded. "I think I can dig up a few things that might help. I'll drop them by if I can find them."

"Great. The simpler the better. I don't need to write any college term papers or anything."

He laughed. "I know what you mean. No, if I can find it, I've got some stuff that's pretty basic. High school notebooks, things like that. From voc ag."

"High school?" she questioned, surprise and laughter mixed in her voice. "You kept your notes from high school?"

He moved in his chair. "I guess that does sound strange. I never throw anything out. So sue me," he said laughing. Suddenly he cocked his head and looked at Katie. "Hey, if you'd taken that course back in high school, you would've been all set. I guess that wouldn't have gone over so well, though. Let's see, how did it go? The boys took voc ag and the girls, homemaking?"

"And from the way people act around here, nothing's changed much," Katie said matter-of-factly.

David was tapping his spoon lightly on the tablecloth. He avoided her gaze. "So, you've been running into a little resistance?"

"Well, maybe I'm getting paranoid in my old age, but I seem to be getting a lot of strange looks. Word sure travels fast around here. Nobody's actually said anything except for Otto Struebler and . . ."

She hesitated for just a second and David added quickly, "Me?"

Katie smiled. "Well, actually I was going to say Ron Hemmingford, but . . . now that you mention it."

David was engrossed in tracing the pattern on the tablecloth. "I've been meaning to talk to you about that. You surprised me that day. It never crossed my mind that you might actually farm the place yourself."

Katie found herself enjoying David's discomfort. "And you laughed because the idea was so ridiculous. Right?"

He was working hard at his tracing. "I guess that's the way it struck me at the time." He stopped with his hand and looked straight at her. "But that was before I really got to know you."

Katie suddenly felt strangely warm all over. She wondered if her face was as red as it felt. "So you don't really think it's all that crazy?"

His answer came in a voice so low and husky she had to strain to hear him. "I'm beginning to think you can do just about anything you set your mind to."

"I'm not interrupting anything, am I?" Gram was back. "You two young people look so serious." Katie arched her eyebrows. *I'm going to have to talk to my grandmother about her timing,* she thought.

They left the club, and Katie practically floated out to the car. She leaned back in the seat, feeling warm and contented and suddenly so sure of herself. Was it the wine? No, of course not. One glass of wine had never affected her this way. She was tipsy with his words, which were still ringing in her head. Not just what he had said, but the way he had said it, his sincerity, the sound of his voice. Little did she know then how much she would need those words. For his part, David was like the little boy whose botched job of mending the shattered cookie jar has finally been discovered and forgiven. He was tired of feeling guilty for what he had said. He had regretted those quick words on the road that day the second they were out of his mouth, but he didn't know how to call them back. Tonight, he had finally found a way. A weight had been lifted, and he felt strangely euphoric.

The ride home was a quiet one. So quiet that Gram fretted in the backseat. *Everything was going so well,* she thought. *I just knew it was too good to last. Something happened while I was gone; I just knew it would. I can't leave those two alone for five minutes before they're at each other's throats.* But how could she know that mere words would only spoil the perfect moment? It didn't take her long to get the picture, though. Once home, David strode quickly around the car, opened Katie's door, took her hand as she stepped out, and guided her toward the door with an arm lightly circling her waist. Once at the door, Katie's eyebrows raised in mock reproach and she whispered, "What about Gram?"

"Oh, no," he blurted, and hurried back to the car as Mrs. Pitcher was struggling out of the backseat.

"I guess I know who counts around here," she chided playfully as she took his arm for support.

Minutes later, David was driving slowly up the road toward his house. His head was spinning. He didn't know whether to trust his feelings. *I know one thing, I've never met anyone like her,* he thought. *She seems so certain of herself, but still she has a softness about her.* He thought of the red dress then. The first time he'd seen her in a dress, and he hoped not the last. Until tonight, it had been jeans and baggy sweatshirts or a sweater and slacks at Otis and Becky's party. Not that he had anything against a pair of tight jeans, especially the way Katie looked in them, but they couldn't hold a candle to that red dress. He pictured the smooth skin of her neck and her face, skin that flushed so easily when she was angry, or even embarrassed. He slammed on his brakes just in time. He had forgotten to punch the button to raise the garage door.

Katie lay snug in bed, smiling up at the ceiling, replaying the evening in her mind. She remembered the way he had looked at her across the table. *Is that the look Gram's been going on about? Where have I been? How come I never noticed it before?* Her smile turned devilish as she thought of his awkward apology and then forgetting Gram in the car. She sighed contentedly. *Thank heaven for killer red dresses. Whoever said Friday the thirteenth is unlucky?*

Just two hundred forty miles away in Rockford, Illinois, with just fifteen minutes left of that Friday the thirteenth, Steve Prescott finished packing. He set his alarm for an early hour. He wanted to be in Willow Grove as early as possible. He smiled to himself in anticipation of the reunion.

Chapter Ten

Katie and her grandmother sat extra long over breakfast the next morning. Both had a second cup of coffee, and Katie even poured a third for herself. She had been chattering like a magpie since first stepping into the kitchen. Making up for all that quiet on the ride home last night, Gram decided. Not that she minded. No, not in the least. She was always glad to see her granddaughter happy, especially now, when she knew the reason. *I ought to know the reason,* she thought. *Haven't I been trying to get something going between the two of them for a good month now? It's high time. I was about to give it up as a lost cause.* She couldn't help smiling, at her plot, which finally seemed to be working, sure, but also as she watched her lovable granddaughter, the world's worst morning person, carrying on so at breakfast, of all things.

She prattled on about the club, the food, the service, David's car, his driving, his voice, his smile, his eyes, his sport coat, the moon, the stars. Gram thought they'd be at the table until lunchtime at this rate, but Katie finally wound down. They went to their Saturday morning housecleaning chores. Three times Katie stopped the noisy vacuum to look out the window. She thought she heard a car. She fixed grilled cheese sandwiches for lunch, and Gram was almost afraid to come to the table. She might be stuck there for the afternoon. But there was no repeat of

101

the breakfast filibuster. Katie jumped up during lunch to check out the window again.

"What is wrong with you?" Gram asked.

"Nothing. I just thought I heard something."

"Are you expecting David maybe?"

"No, why would you say that?" Katie asked as she sat back down.

"Oh, just a wild guess."

Katie shot a quick glance across the table. "Well, he did say he had some things for me to read if he could find them. I thought he might drop by."

Gram swallowed the last of her sandwich. "Not a bad guess, since he drops by just about every day."

"Oh, he does not. Besides, he just stops to check on you."

"Uh-huh," Gram said innocently. "You mean the same old woman he left locked in the backseat of the car last night while he followed Miss Red Dress to the door?"

"Oh, you," Katie said, as she tried to keep from laughing. "He just wanted to help us into the house one at a time."

"Yes, that must have been it," Gram said sarcastically.

The two cleaned up the kitchen, and Katie lugged the vacuum upstairs to do her bedroom. She was on her hands and knees, pushing the wand as far under her bed as she could reach. Her head was close to the noisy machine, but she thought she heard her name. She punched the off button.

"Katie!" Gram shouted from the stairs.

"Yes!" Katie shouted back.

"There's someone down here to see you."

Katie smiled smugly at herself in the mirror over the dresser. She ran her fingers lightly through her hair to fluff it, and grabbed her lipstick for a quick touch-up. A careful smoothing of her red sweatshirt and a tug on her tight jeans, and she was ready. She skipped lightly down the stairs and swung around the corner on the way to the kitchen. That's when she saw what struck her as odd. Her grandmother was standing by the table looking strangely uncomfortable. The whole scene really had no time to register in her brain before she breezed through the door and came face-to-face with—Steve Prescott.

"What are you doing here?" she practically shrieked.

"Well, that's some fine greeting," he said, obviously disappointed. "You got my card, didn't you?"

Katie vowed on the spot never to throw away mail unopened again. "Of course," she answered truthfully, though only technically so. "I just didn't think you'd be here so soon." This guy doesn't seem to understand the spoken or the written language, she thought. Now what?

"I wanted to get here as soon as I could. Hey, it's Valentine's Day," he added, gesturing with a huge heart-shaped box of candy in one hand and a long plastic-wrapped bouquet of red and white carnations in the other.

"You didn't have to go to all this trouble," she said.

"What? You think I'd let Valentine's Day go by without seeing my girl? Here." He handed her the candy and flowers.

Katie was still cringing at his "my girl" greeting. She took the gifts awkwardly, put the enormous red heart box of candy on the table and handed the flowers to her grandmother, who busied herself searching for a vase. Steve stepped toward Katie and wrapped her in an embrace before she knew what was happening. "Happy Valentine's Day, darling," he said. "I've missed you." It sounded to Katie like something he'd been rehearsing in the car. She knew he'd never called her darling before, that was for sure. She was afraid any minute he was going to bow and kiss her hand.

That's when Katie made her big mistake. She should have sent him packing right then. While his car was still warm. Loaded his flowers and candy and all back into that car and sent him down the road in the same direction he'd come from. It would have been far easier on him in the long run. And on her too, that's for sure. But no, she couldn't do that. She was much too thoughtful, much too gracious, much too hospitable for such necessary rudeness. After all, hadn't he driven two hundred forty miles just to see her? She was thinking like her grandmother now, not exactly surprising, since she'd probably inherited such gentle traits from her anyway.

So plain old Willow Grove, small-town, farm-country neighborliness took over. And, of course, it was all misunderstood by Steve Prescott. What he needed was "it's been nice knowing you, but . . ." What he got instead was encouragement. Katie finally remembered she hadn't introduced Steve to her grandmother. With that formality out of the way, the two women worked as a team. Gram took care of her specialty—a generous slice of fresh apple pie with a mug of coffee to top off whatever Steve had been able to grab along the way. Katie took his coat and busied herself arranging the carnations in the vase Gram had found. She centered the finished arrangement on the table, right next to the colossal red heart box of candy. To make room, she had to move David's red roses, full, velvety blossoms now, to the counter by the stove. Then she swallowed hard, trying to forget such words as *darling* and *favorite girl,* and sat at the table to catch up on the news from school. She'd get rid of him as soon as she could, but she couldn't be rude. In fact, she was so busy trying to be friendly and neighborly, she didn't hear or see a certain blue pickup drive into the yard.

David got out of his truck slowly, studying the silver Nissan with the Illinois plates. He cradled a small stack of reading material in his left arm as he headed for the door. Sugar trotted by his side, soothed by the familiar voice. He opened the metal storm door, tapped lightly on the heavy oak door, pushed it open as had become his custom in the last several weeks, and stepped inside. From where she sat at the end of the table, Katie could see down the hall toward the door. She jerked her head toward the door at the sound of the familiar tapping and then looked up in horror as David stepped inside. Why she should be so shocked, even she couldn't imagine. After all, she'd been expecting him all day. She jumped up and actually considered running to her room and never coming out again, but decided that really wouldn't solve anything. David walked into the kitchen and took in the whole scene with one quick glance—a stranger with his mouth full of pie, the red heart-shaped box of candy, the vase of red and white carnations, even his own red roses consigned to the counter by the spice rack.

If he hadn't already jumped to some serious conclusions with that one glance, he was dangerously close to it. One look at his face usually gave him away, and if that didn't do it, there was always the tone of his voice. And now that voice was as cold as it had been warm the night before. "Excuse me. I didn't know I was interrupting." He plopped the stack of books onto the table. "I just wanted to drop these off. I can see you're busy." He would have turned and walked back out the door if Katie hadn't grabbed his arm.

"No, no, that's okay," she said. Now she stood behind her chair, her arms folded awkwardly across her chest. She was wishing the floor might open up and swallow her. How could she explain that there wasn't anything to explain when she couldn't even seem to get that point across to Steve? She tried, but it all came out wrong, and Steve wasn't any help. No, he wasn't any help at all. "We were just talking about school. Well, Steve was eating. I mean, he hadn't had dessert." She was babbling, and, as usual, she couldn't seem to do anything about it. "Oh, you haven't met Steve, have you? Well, no, how *would* you have met him? Steve, this is our neighbor David Cairn, from just up the road. David, this is Steve Prescott, a friend from the school where I teach, or where I used to teach, I guess I should say.'' She smiled weakly. ''He just dropped in this morning.'' She was looking to her grandmother for help. ''Took us by surprise, didn't he, Gram?'' *Took us by surprise?* she thought to herself. *More like struck us dead in our tracks.*

Steve set down his fork and reached out to shake hands. ''Hia. Nice to meet you.''

David studied him with narrowed eyes. *Kind of short. Who's he trying to impress with that handshake? Probably a lifter. I bet he's some kind of coach. Wrestling. Yep, I bet he's a wrestling coach. He must not be able to see his own hands without those glasses.*

Steve withstood the scrutiny with a defiant look of his own. ''Don't believe a word of all that,'' he said. ''I didn't just drop in. Nobody just drops in on February fourteenth.'' He gestured toward the flowers and the candy on the table in front of him. ''Say, I'm glad you're here, you being a farmer and all. Maybe you can set me straight on something. I've been hearing a lot of crazy talk from my girl since she came out here. She's got some wild dream about being a farmer.'' He laughed. ''Can you believe it? She wants to farm this place all by herself. Have you ever heard anything crazier than that?''

David felt a dull anger growing inside him. *What about last night? Didn't last night mean anything to her at all? And this guy. She never mentioned she had someone back at school.* Deep inside, he knew he was being unreasonable, but he couldn't stop himself. He leaned both hands on the back of the chair and eyed Katie calmly. ''No, as a matter of fact, I don't think I have,'' he said evenly.

She turned toward him, a questioning look in her eyes. ''What!'' she blurted. She was remembering what he had said last night. Was he lying then?

But Steve interrupted with entirely too much excitement. "See, what did I tell you? Isn't that exactly what I've been saying all along? Give up all this silly business and get back in the classroom, where you belong. There's no way you're going to become a farmer." He had no clue about the drama building around him.

David watched her face closely. He couldn't resist one more shot. "That's what people around here think too. They're all expecting her to fall flat on her face." He knew exactly what he was doing to her fragile confidence, but he felt a strange satisfaction as he watched her neck redden and the color slowly work its way up to her cheeks. But then he saw her eyes. He hadn't bargained on the hurt he saw in her eyes. He had seen anger there before, had even been the cause of it, but he had never seen the hurt. A sick feeling washed over him.

Mrs. Pitcher was attacking the counter with a sponge. He'd upset her too. Even Mr. Valentine from Illinois knew enough to keep quiet for a change. He was busy again with his pie. David waited for Katie to strike out as she had before. He expected it. In fact, he wanted it. He hoped that a flash of her red-haired temper would even the score somehow, make him feel better.

"I think you'd better go." That was all she said.

He turned without a word and stalked for the door. *Come on, come on, shout at me, stamp your foot, do something.* But then he was outside in the bright sun. Even the dog sat solemnly in the doorway of her little house, watching his retreat down the porch steps. So it was going to be the silent treatment all around, and that was making him feel worse than any words ever could.

He climbed into his truck and headed for home. He was deep in his thoughts, but not the happy ones of the night before. He had hurt her. He had let his anger get the better of him. What a stupid thing to say, especially when he didn't even mean it. Nobody around here was thinking anything like that except maybe for Otto, and he didn't count. He knew where she was vulnerable. He knew how afraid she was of failing. And he took advantage of that fear. He felt horrible. He had made too much of last night; that was the problem. What was he expecting anyway? They'd had dinner together. So what! You can't make any kind of commitment out of that. And she never mentioned this guy from Illinois, but then why should she? No, now he knew the truth. The problem was all in his own mind. He thought he had sensed something between them, something to build on. Even that very first night, more than a month ago, when he had seen her walk through the door, he had felt something special, and he thought she had felt it too. And Otis! What about him and that craziness about the way she was looking at him? No, he had imagined it all. There was never anything between them except friendship. And now even that was gone. He had acted like a fool.

As the door closed after him, Katie burst into tears and ran to her room. Steve turned in his chair and looked to Mrs. Pitcher. ''What in the heck is going on around here, anyway?''

She pulled out a chair and sat next to him. ''Let me see if I can explain it to you, Mr. Prescott.''

Katie sobbed quietly into her pillow. Her thoughts were a confused mess. *What a horrible, horrible man. How could he say such things? And after last night. I hate him.* It was even worse when she thought about his exact words. She shivered. *Is that really what people are saying? They expect to see me make a fool of myself? Lose everything? And he must think I won't disappoint them.* She tensed her body with a fresh thought. *He wants to be there to snap up this farm. I just know it. That's why he's been pretending to help. He wants me to fail just as much as anyone. More. I hate him.* Suddenly she remembered Steve, and she groaned. *What am I going to do with him? He's an okay friend, but that's as far as I want it to go. I've got to tell him. That's all there is to it. It's not fair to lead him on. What am I saying, I haven't led him on. I've tried to tell him. The problem is, he won't listen.* Suddenly she felt a hand on her shoulder. She pulled her face out of the pillow and saw Gram standing there.

Gram sat on the edge of the bed and put an arm around her granddaughter. Katie sank her head onto her grandmother's bony shoulder. "What am I going to do?" she pleaded. "I've made a mess of everything."

"There, there," Gram said softly. "Everything will be just fine."

"But you heard what he said. I'm the laughingstock of the whole town."

"I don't believe that for a minute," Gram answered. "For one thing, I refuse to believe most people in Willow Grove even know what you're doing. How would they?"

Katie straightened up and wiped her eyes on the sleeve of her sweatshirt. "But why would he say those things?"

"He was angry, dear. Don't you see? He has as much of a temper as you. He just has a different way of showing it. You shout and stamp your foot. He blurts out the most hurtful thing he can think of, even if it isn't true."

"I think he wants this farm. Didn't he say so himself that day I went to see Mr. Peters? He thinks if I lose everything, he can buy it up from the bank."

Gram shook her head and smiled. "You're imagining things, dear. Do you really want to know why he acted the way he did today?" Katie looked at her grandmother, waiting for more. "Well, I'll tell you. He's jealous."

Katie shook her head. "You're not going to start with that love theory of yours again, are you? You almost had me believing it last night." She turned back toward her grandmother with an agonized look on her face. "He was so wonderful last night, and now today he's just a different person. I swear, he's like Dr. Jekyll or Mr. Hyde. Which one was the bad one anyway? I always forget.''

Gram laughed. ''I don't know.'' Then she grew serious and put her hand on Katie's shoulder. ''Now listen to me, 'cause I know what I'm talking about. David has got a grade A, number-one case of jealousy. Why, it was plain to see the minute he walked in the door. He turned every shade of green when he saw Mr. Prescott sitting in our kitchen. And heaven knows your friend from Illinois didn't help matters. Why he even had me believing we had a wedding to plan for.''

''Oh, please!'' Katie rolled her eyes. ''Like that will ever happen! That man takes politeness as some kind of declaration of love.'' Suddenly she jumped to her feet. ''Oh, gee, I forgot about him. Gram, what am I going to do with him?''

Her grandmother smiled. ''Sit down, dear. It's all taken care of.'' She reached over and patted Katie's arm. ''I don't think that young man will be bothering you again.'' She covered a giggle with her hand. ''I even kept the flowers and candy.''

''How did you do it? I just hated to be mean. He came so far.''

''Oh, don't worry about hurting men's feelings so much. Aren't they supposed to be the stronger sex? At least that's what they like to tell us. Well, give them a chance to prove it once in a while. If they need a good bop over the head now and again to shape them up, then do it for them. They'll bounce back. Your Mr. Prescott left here thinking he'd had an enjoyable little drive, and he'd get to see everything he'd missed on the other side of the highway driving back home. And don't forget, he got a piece of my apple pie, didn't he?''

Katie smiled for the first time in the last thirty minutes. ''Oh, you! How do you know so much?''

"You mean about men? I didn't live fifty-two years with your grandfather without learning something."

"Well, maybe so, but I still think you're wrong about Dr. Jekyll."

Chapter Eleven

In the weeks that followed, Katie had plenty of time to think about her grandmother's assessment of men, and of David Cairn in particular. She still wasn't buying the theory that jealousy was at the root of his bad manners. Nor was she likely to have a chance to explore that theory firsthand, because David hadn't shown his face since that unforgettable St. Valentine's Day. Not that she was out looking for him. The fact is, she was dreading a face-to-face meeting. Why, just two days earlier she was on her way to visit Becky and drove right past the Skibby place when she saw David's truck parked in front of the garage. She knew she was being juvenile, but she just couldn't help herself.

She and Becky were becoming good friends. Becky had come along just at the right time for Katie. She maintained two or three long-distance telephone friendships with teachers back in Illinois. But they were still just that—long-distance, and anyway, she was already an outsider there. Strange, she thought, that she could be an outsider in the life she had just left as well as in this new life, but she was. She needed someone near her own age to feel comfortable with over coffee, and that's exactly how she felt around Becky. Besides, the two were ideally suited for one another. They were both outsiders of sorts. And certainly Becky's dream of becoming a nurse was almost as outlandish, given her troubled background, as Katie's plan of jumping from a teacher's desk to a tractor. Becky was good for Katie's confidence. She was so excited about the idea of planting seeds and watching a whole field of corn grow because of something you had done. She put it in such a simple way that Katie had to laugh. "I can remember my real mama used to love to work in the garden," was the way she said it. "Just think, that's what you're gonna be doin', only it's a real big garden."

The weather turned cold the first of March, just when everyone was beginning to think of spring. Katie was making progress in her self-taught course on becoming a farmer. The books David had dropped on the table before things turned ugly were actually helping. They were basic enough to answer some questions Katie would have thought too stupid to ask anyone. She took delivery of her seed corn and found she could manage the sacks well enough. Not that she could toss them around, but she would be able to get them from the truck to the planter without doing serious damage to her back. She had already decided to use fertilizer in bulk form, so she wouldn't have additional sacks to lug.

The first real physical sacrifice to her new chosen profession, with the exception of a few aches and pains from climbing around the machinery, was her fingernails. She broke one nail down to the quick hitching the corn planter to the tractor. And all she was doing was moving the planter to the front of the machine shed so she could investigate it under one of the big overhead lights. That night she took clippers to the rest of her pride and joy, reducing them to a reasonable length. She had been nursing those nails for years, and felt like crying as she examined her newly shorn digits. She made a promise that she would pamper herself with a professional manicure, complete with the best set of applied nails she could buy, when the harvest was done in the fall. Then she slipped into town for a hair appointment. She needed a shorter style, so her hair wouldn't be getting in the way, and she was happy with what the stylist came up with. It would take her a while to get used to the new look, though.

So things were taking shape. Katie had even sketched diagrams of each of her fields, showing what direction she would plant and what needed to be done before the planting actually started. She was getting excited. Oh, sure, she was still scared out of her wits, but she was ready to try this thing. She just knew she'd feel better when it all started for real. So what happened? It snowed. Spring was less than a week away on the calendar, but winter wasn't about to give up. This snow was so heavy and wet it caused some tree damage, and brought down power lines. Katie and Gram were without electricity for more than twenty-four hours.

Katie took the four-wheel drive to town as soon as the roads were passable. They needed groceries, as usual. She walked through the door of the supermarket to a wild scene. It looked like the whole town was shopping. In fact, she got the last grocery cart in the rack. *What is this?* she wondered. *Did everyone run out of food at the same time or what? This is going to take forever.* Lines of loaded carts snaked from each of the checkout stands partway down the grocery aisles. She'd never seen the likes of that around this small town. But the laughter and chatter were contagious, with everyone sharing snow stories. A good snowstorm brings out the best in everyone, Katie thought.

She nodded and smiled her way in and around carts, through the canned vegetable section, wheeled around the corner on her way to the breakfast cereals, and smacked head-on into David's cart.

"Whoops," Katie said, "sorry about that." She knew her face was already red.

"No problem," he answered, and then his face brightened as recognition sunk in. "Oh, hi." He studied her face. "What did you do to your hair?"

She ran a hand self-consciously through her sheared locks. "Oh, I just wanted to try something new. For the summer, you know."

"I like it. Well, it was nice the other way too, but this is . . . cute." Now it was his turn to be embarrassed.

"Thanks."

Now he avoided her eyes. "Quite a crowd, huh?"

They had to stand there for a long moment cart to cart, because he was boxed in by other shoppers. "How's your grandmother getting along?"

"Oh, she's just fine." She was supposed to be mad at the guy, and here she was making small talk. And after the things he'd said. She had even planned what she would say to him if she ever had the chance, but now seeing him, it was all out the window.

"Were your lights out long?" he asked.

She smiled at the question. They lived half a mile apart, so they likely shared the same power outage problems. "Oh, about twenty-four hours," she answered.

"Yeah, same with me. You have any trouble staying warm?"

"No, we have a gas space heater. You?"

"No. Fireplace." He moved his cart to let two shoppers pass. "Guess I'm kind of in the way here." The traffic cleared a little and he started to go by, but stopped suddenly. "I—I—" he stammered. "I didn't mean those things I said." He looked like he wanted to say more except for the crush of shoppers. "Well, I'll be talking to you."

"Right." Stunned and suddenly elated, she watched him as he moved past. That was an apology, wasn't it? Any remaining anger just drained away at his simple words. He was wearing a brown ski jacket that she suddenly thought made him look squeezable like a brown teddy bear. And he had a stocking cap perched high on his head. She smiled. She was almost certain a moment ago his eyes brightened for just a second when he first recognized her as the driver of the other cart. Was it just shock at the hair, or was it because he was glad to see her? *I can't believe he noticed my hair,* she thought to herself with a grin.

Katie stopped by to see Becky the morning of the twenty-first, the first official day of spring, and the weather was actually acting like it. As she walked out to the garage, she breathed deeply. Spring in the country. She hadn't smelled that clean, delightful smell in years. The snow was melting fast now. She could see huge patches of black in the fields, where the dirt showed through. Becky was uncharacteristically jumpy as they sipped coffee at the kitchen table. She was usually a model of calmness, but not today. She was up looking out the window one minute or nervously checking the baby in her playpen the next. She tried to add more coffee to Katie's cup, which was already full to the top.

"What is wrong with you today?"

She put the coffeepot back on the stove. "Nothing. Why?"

"Because you're acting as nervous as a cow in a—what is it Otis says?" They both laughed.

"Oh, I don't know," Becky said. "He says the strangest things."

Katie took a sip of her coffee. "So? I'm waiting. Is it Lena or what?"

"Oh, no, she's just fine. It's nothing like that." Becky took a deep breath. "I—I do have something important to tell you, and a big, big favor to ask."

Katie looked concerned. "You know I'd be glad to help any way I can. What is it?"

Becky ran a forefinger around the brim of her cup, her head down. "Otis and me are getting married."

Katie had her cup halfway to her mouth. She set it back down untouched. "What do you mean you're getting married? You're not already married?"

Becky shook her head. "No, we've been calling ourselves Mr. and Mrs., but it just isn't so."

"But I thought Otis said . . ."

"I know. We decided to tell everyone we were married when Lena and me joined him here. Everyone back home already knew we weren't. We started living together after he got out of the hospital. We planned to do it up proper when Lena came along last year, but . . ." She rested her chin in the palm of one hand. "Otis doesn't have a family, and my papa and that woman he's married to, they made it mighty plain they didn't want to be a part of whatever we were plannin'."

"Even with such a beautiful grandchild?" Katie asked, looking toward the playpen.

Becky raised her head and looked at Katie. Tears welled in her eyes. "I'm tellin' you the gospel truth. Papa's never laid eyes on that little baby. I know it's *her* fault, my stepmother. I heard she's been tellin' around that Lena's no granddaughter to her, and she doesn't want a little brat callin' her grandma."

Katie reached over and touched Becky's arm. "I'm sorry."

She straightened in her chair. "Well, it's all water under the bridge now anyway. All I know is they don't know what they're missing not lovin' that beautiful little baby."

"Listen," Katie said with a sudden idea, "Lena's already got her own grandmother right down the road from here. Gram's just crazy about her. You know she's hoping you get that job at the hospital so she can take care of her. Besides, she loves to be called grandma."

Becky smiled through her tears. "I know. She's too wonderful for words. Otis says she's a saint on earth, for sure. Lena calls her Goom already. I know it's cause she's heard you calling her Gram. She stands looking out that front window, and when a car goes by, she says, 'Goom come?'" They both laughed.

Katie clapped her hands. "So, you're getting married. That's wonderful news. Now why would you be nervous to tell me that?"

Becky opened her eyes wide in a look of doubt. "You haven't heard everything yet. I haven't asked you the big favor."

"Well, whatever it is, I'm sure the answer will be yes."

"I hope so." She clasped both hands around her coffee mug. "I was wondering if you'd be my maid of honor?"

Katie's mouth gaped in surprise. "Why, I'd love to." Her eyes glistened. "I would consider it an honor."

Becky heaved a sigh of relief. "Oh, you don't know how happy that makes me. We haven't known each other very long, and I was afraid you might think I was imposin'. But already I consider you my best friend. To tell the truth, you're kinda like what I thought an older sister would be like."

Katie brushed away a tear. "That's so nice of you to say. But what do you mean by older?" she added with a grin.

"Oh, no, I didn't mean nothing by that," Becky said quickly. "It's just that I always dreamed if I had a sister, some day we'd sit around my kitchen drinking coffee and talking about all kinds of things." She held out her hands. "And that's what we do."

"Well, to tell the truth, I always wanted a sister too," said Katie. "I used to be so jealous of my friends who had brothers or sisters." She hesitated. "So when is the big event? Tell me everything."

"Well, there isn't really much to tell. It's just going to be real small. We already worked it out with Reverend Hargstrom for a week from Saturday." She added quickly, "I know that's not giving much notice, but once we decided on it, we just wanted to go ahead as fast as we could. If you've got something else planned, both Otis and me would understand, being as how we asked you so late and all.''

"No, no, that's fine. I don't have another thing on my calendar. And even if I did, it wouldn't be half as important as your wedding.''

"Da! Da!'' Lena was standing in her playpen in the living room.

Becky jumped up and looked out the kitchen window. "I swear, she doesn't miss a thing. Otis just drove in. How she would know that was him I declare I don't know.''

A moment later the porch door slammed shut and then the kitchen door swung open and Otis stepped inside. "Hello, neighbor,'' he drawled, nodding at Katie. She returned his greeting.

"I've got some extra coffee. Want a cup?'' Becky asked.

"Don't mind if I do.'' He pushed his cowboy hat back on his head and peeked around the corner into the living room. Lena jumped up and down in the playpen. "How's my little punkin?'' She rattled the sides of the playpen in answer. "Now just hold on a minute, little girl, till I git outta these muddy boots.'' He grinned at Katie and Becky. "We been movin' cattle. More like playin' in the mud.'' He pulled off the boots and dumped them on a rug by the door, then made a beeline for Lena, to rescue her from the playpen before sitting at the table.

"Otis, you'll get her all muddy. And be careful of this hot coffee,'' Becky warned as she placed a cup near him.

"I'll watch her close.'' He balanced the baby on his knee and took a careful sip of his coffee. "So what've you two hens been cluckin' about?''

Becky grinned proudly. "I asked her, and she said yes.''

"That's mighty fine,'' Otis said. "Well, I did my part too. Dave said he'd be glad to be my best man.''

Katie choked on a fresh sip of coffee and needed a slap on the back to help stop the coughing. The thought of standing so close to David through a wedding ceremony left her head in a whirl. Besides, she still didn't know for certain how things stood between them. She hadn't seen him since the grocery store. But he had apologized, hadn't he? She thought so.

Gram was on the phone in thirty seconds when Katie told her the news about the wedding. First to tell Becky how happy she was, and next to invite her over to talk dresses. Becky came that very evening, alone; she had left Otis at home to baby-sit. Gram was unhappy about that. She'd grown even more attached to little Lena, if that was possible, since she'd heard the Goom story.

Katie had dragged her wedding attendant dresses out of the closet for the three to inspect. She had been in five weddings back in Rockford and had taken each dress home to the farm because of limited space in her apartment. To be honest, she doubted she would ever wear them again.

Becky was shocked when she saw the pretty gowns arranged neatly on an ironing caddy in the living room. "Oh, no, I couldn't wear one of those pretty dresses," she protested. "That just wouldn't be right. These dresses are yours."

"That's silly," Katie said. "I wore each of them one time, and I can't imagine when I'll ever wear them again."

Becky's eyes glowed as she looked at the colorful finery. "I was just planning on a plain dress. I never dreamed of anything so fancy."

"A girl only gets married once in her lifetime," Gram announced solemnly. "At least we hope so," she said as she pursed her lips and squinted at the two young women. "So she has every right to look her best." She adjusted one of the dresses on its hanger. "Now which of these do you like?"

Becky sorted slowly through the lot. Finally, she pulled a cream-colored one off the caddy and held it at arm's length. It was a scoop-necked affair with flouncy sleeves.

It had always been one of Katie's favorites. "Oh, this one is so pretty. If you don't think it's improper," she said with a flush of embarrassment in her white cheeks. "It being almost white and all."

"Stuff and nonsense," said Gram. "That's just some silly old superstition. You can wear anything you please."

Katie stared at her grandmother and fought to keep a straight face. She distinctly remembered a dinner conversation several years earlier in which Gram had expressed a completely different opinion. Oh, the times they are a-changin', she thought to herself.

Gram held the dress up in front of Becky. "That will work just fine. We'll have to tuck here and there." She narrowed her eyes, appraising the situation. "We're going to have to get you fattened up. A good wind comes along, and you'll be blown away. Let's see now. I think if we take it up about two inches, it'll be just perfect. Becky, go into my bedroom there and try it on. Katie, get my pin box from the sewing room. We've got some work to do."

It was Saturday, April first, the day of the wedding. Gram was up to her tricks, as usual. She had made plans for the best man to pick up the groom at eight o'clock (the wedding was at ten). "You just get him out of the house," she ordered David over the phone, "and give us some time to work. But don't be late to the church. Understand?"

Then Katie and Gram swooped into the Skibby homestead at just after eight and found things to their liking. Otis was off with the best man, Becky was in her robe, and baby Lena was playing in the living room. "Goom," she shouted as they came in the door, and she toddled after Gram wherever she went, but her "help" didn't bother the pair in the least. First they used a curling iron to give Becky's dark hair a little body. Next, Gram worked on her nails, and Katie put some color in her face with a light blush and a pastel lip gloss. Finally, Katie went to work on her dark brown eyes, highlighting them just right. "There," she said as she stepped back and surveyed her work like a painter studying her canvas, "just perfect. See what you think."

Becky hurried to a mirror. "I can't believe that's really me. I wonder what Otis will think?"

"He's going to love it," said Gram, "or he'll hear from me. Now, hurry and get your dress on, so we can comb out your hair. And don't get any of that makeup on that lovely dress."

Katie and her grandmother waited anxiously in the living room for the final appearance. Katie had been so rushed, she hadn't had time to worry about spending a good part of the day beside David. That is, she hadn't had time to worry today. But she'd gotten in plenty of worry time during the past week. She reminded herself that he had been more than civil in the grocery store, and she wouldn't expect him to be anything less than that at a wedding, of all things. Just try to be congenial, she reminded herself.

The door opened and Becky came out. "Well, look at you!" said Gram. "I declare, you're pretty as a picture." She studied the bride carefully. "Just one thing missing."

"What's that?" asked Becky with a look of alarm.

"You need something for your throat, with that neckline." She slipped her hand in her pocket and brought out a small box. "I think this will do just fine." She snapped open the box to reveal a tiny silver cross on a thin silver chain. "My dear husband gave this to me for our first Christmas. I've treasured it for years, but I just don't have a thing to wear it with."

Becky was overcome. "Oh, Mrs. Pitcher, I couldn't possibly accept such a wonderful gift. It's much too precious."

"Nonsense. I want you to have it. Katie, would you help with this? My eyes are letting me down just now."

Katie took the delicate cross and chain from her grandmother and slipped it around Becky's neck. She had trouble with the clasp herself, because she found her eyes misty at the thought that she finally really did have a sister.

"No sniffling now, you two," ordered Gram. "We don't have time to fix your eyes all over again."

Becky hugged Gram. "Thank you, Mrs. Pitcher."

"Goom," shouted Lena, pointing with one of her Legos.

"I mean Goom," said Becky, and they all laughed.

Katie was surprised to see a modest crowd already waiting inside the little church when they arrived, but not half as surprised as Becky. "What are all these people doing here?" Becky whispered. "We didn't invite anyone."

"Don't look at me," Gram declared. "I think a certain Mr. Cairn had something to do with it, and I think he has something else up his sleeve too. Just you wait."

As Katie took in the scene, she could tell that most of the fifteen or twenty guests were the neighbors who had attended the housewarming. *What a thoughtful touch,* she decided. *Even my friend Otto is here, I see.* Gram let Lena toddle slowly up the aisle to the approving smiles of the neighbors, and they took their place in the first pew. Katie glanced over at Becky, who was nervously pacing. *I hope she doesn't back out now,* she thought. That would be an interesting twist, wouldn't it?

As they waited, David and Otis filed solemnly out from behind the altar, accompanied by Reverend Hargstrom, and the three stood together just inside the sanctuary. Katie's eyes locked on David, looking positively handsome in a beautiful dark suit. He had that unruly shock of hair brushed neatly in place, and he looked absolutely—what was the word she was looking for—*devastating*? Oh, well, that will have to do, she thought. *Calm down, girl,* she reminded herself. *I'm not sure how we're going to hit it off today. Only time will tell.*

Katie's eyes drifted to Otis and she smiled. She couldn't help it; it looked so strange to see him in a suit. *He is really a handsome man,* she thought, *but what a shame he looks so much older than his age.* His hair was slicked back on the sides, and it struck her that he looked like a different person without his cowboy hat. He had lost his wild, untamed look. *That hat is really a part of his personality,* she decided.

Reverend Hargstrom nodded ever so slightly, and the tiny church was suddenly filled with organ music from the loft above and behind the guests. "Music too?" Becky said quietly. "This is more than I ever could have hoped for."

Katie put a hand on Becky's arm. "That's just Mrs. Wise. She wouldn't dream of letting a wedding take place without music." Katie smiled. "Well, are you ready, little sister? Let's get this show on the road." She started the slow walk down the aisle. *We never practiced this, but I guess I've done it enough times,* she thought. *Always a bridesmaid, never a bride, as the old saying goes.*

David watched Katie make her way up the aisle. As a matter of fact, he had seen no one else since he and Otis had come out from behind the altar. It was hard to miss her anyway with that bright red hair, but today she was something special. Maybe it was the way her off-the-shoulder emerald-green dress showed off that hair. But what did he know? He wasn't into women's fashions, but he knew what he liked. And he definitely liked what he saw today. He knew he needed his head examined for not following up after the thaw at the grocery store, but he wasn't sure what his status was. He couldn't forget the wrestler from Illinois. He suddenly took two or three steps toward her as she neared the altar, and offered his arm.

As she took it, he turned to her and said quietly, "Hi, Squirt. Still mad at me?" Katie looked at him sharply and saw a playful grin toying at his mouth.

"Yes," she whispered, and smiled mischievously back at him as she dug her fingernails into the hardness of his arm. She remembered too late that she had been declawed.

As she stood next to David just inside the altar rail, her hand resting lightly on his arm, she almost forgot to watch Becky's trip down the aisle. She recovered herself just in time to see Otis's reaction when he finally saw the "new" Becky close up. Katie hadn't seen the sleepy-eyed cowboy so awake since she'd known him. Katie hated to leave David's side to take her place next to Becky for the actual ceremony. And as Reverend Hargstrom piously intoned the vows, she couldn't stop herself from fantasizing that those timeless words were being spoken about her. "Do you take this woman to be your lawful wedded wife; to have and to hold; for better, for worse; in sickness and in health; for richer, for poorer; forsaking all others; till death do you part?" She was snapped suddenly out of her dreamworld when she heard Otis improvise: "I shore do."

At the close of the ceremony, the minister introduced the couple to the guests. "Ladies and Gentlemen, may I present Mr. and Mrs. Otis Skibby." Katie could tell by Becky's deep sigh that she was relieved it was finally official. Then came the surprise that Gram had hinted at. The minister continued. "Everyone is invited to celebrate with Mr. and Mrs. Skibby at a luncheon at the club immediately following the ceremony." Otis and Becky looked at each other in surprise.

As she joined David for the walk back down the aisle behind the bridal couple, Katie whispered, "Did you have anything to do with that?"

"With what?"

"You know what. With the luncheon?"

"Oh, that. Well, maybe."

"I thought so." She smiled up at him and squeezed his arm. And this time she didn't even miss the fingernails. "That was really nice of you."

He felt a tingling sensation go all the way up his spine to his hairline. *I finally did something right,* he thought.

* * *

The luncheon was a huge success, and Becky and Otis were obviously pleased once they got over their embarrassment at all the attention. Their wedding day had blossomed far beyond their first simple plans. They were becoming more and more at home among these folks, their neighbors. After lunch, David said a few words to congratulate the pair. Then he turned to them with a twinkle in his eye. "We've made reservations for you in Des Moines tonight. And we just happen to have two tickets to the Garth Brooks concert."

Katie knew there was no "we" involved. It was all David, with maybe a little Gram thrown in for good measure. She soon learned the truth of that as David went on. He pulled out his car keys and passed them over to Otis along with an envelope. "Take my car. There's more room. Now get going. You've got some packing to do. Oh, wait a minute, I almost forgot. If you were worrying about little Lena, don't. Mrs. P, better known these days as Goom, has volunteered to keep a close watch on her for the weekend. So go and have fun."

Otis got another chance to give a speech. It was short and sweet, but there could be no doubting his sincerity. "This feller is something else," he said, looking at David and shaking his head in disbelief. "I just don't know what to say."

"Then don't say anything," David broke in. "Go on, get out of here."

Katie had trouble getting to sleep that night. She still had so much to think about. She replayed the wedding all over again in her mind: standing so close to David, listening to the vows, watching Becky's face when the minister pronounced them man and wife, David's generosity to a couple he really hadn't known for long. She lay quietly in the darkness of her room surrounded by these pleasant memories.

Suddenly an irksome thought demanded attention, and she tossed and turned in annoyance. But she couldn't keep the newcomer out. There was nothing to do but face what happened after Otis and Becky left. The group suddenly split as if by some natural law. The women bunched around one of the long tables. The men drifted toward the bar. She reluctantly gave in to this old Willow Grove custom and joined the women. What else could she do? The talk was about babies and clothes and cooking and schools. She knew the men were discussing the weather and especially the upcoming planting season, with maybe a little politics thrown in. She knew better than to join them. She knew from the earlier party that she was definitely an outsider. And besides, such an intrusion would be unthinkable. Otto Struebler would have had a stroke.

She understood at that moment more clearly than she had since this whole business about the farm started that what she was about to do was more than just a physical challenge. She was going against an unspoken rule about the place of men and women. At least in Willow Grove. There might be women doctors and lawyers and chief executives and computer programmers and even astronauts, but not women farmers. Katie knew that the physical demands must have accounted for that over the years, but why now, when every farmer's machine shed was filled with things to make the job easier? *It's probably harder than it looks,* she decided. Well, time will tell.

One worry led to another, and Katie didn't fall asleep for hours. She knew the time for doing was nearly upon her. *Time for me to put my money where my mouth is,* she vowed. The weather had been beautiful for nearly two weeks. She decided Monday was the day.

Chapter Twelve

Sunday afternoon, Katie walked out to the field nearest the house. Her dad had raised corn there the year before, and the browned and broken stalks still showed clearly where the rows had been. She made a wide circuit of the field, checking for wet spots. She found the ground muddy in places but nothing she couldn't walk through, though her hiking boots were caked by the time she reached the house. She did make a mental note of three low areas she would have to avoid.

"Are you sure it's not too early?" asked Gram that evening. Otis and Becky had just stopped by for Lena on their way home from Des Moines, and Goom was missing the little one already.

"No, I don't think so," Katie replied.

"Why haven't we seen anyone else out?"

"I don't really know. Maybe we just haven't noticed."

"Did you ask David? What did the men say the other day?"

Katie was getting exasperated. "Gram, you know very well I don't know what the men said the other day. I was stuck off with the women talking babies. Now, are we going to go through this every time I go to the field?"

Gram grumbled into her needlework.

Katie was up early the next morning. The temperature was in the low thirties, but was expected to rise to sixty by the afternoon. She was so nervous she had trouble forcing down a piece of toast for breakfast.

"That isn't all you're having for breakfast, is it?" asked Gram. She was still out of sorts because she wouldn't be chasing a one-year-old around the house all day. "Your father always ate a full breakfast before he went to the field."

"I'm sorry, Gram, I'm just not very hungry." She grabbed her coat and rushed for the door before her grandmother had a chance to add more. She backed the tractor out of the shed and pulled it up to the fuel tank. After it was filled to the brim, she backed around to the disk, which she had pulled out of the shed several weeks earlier. This time, the hitching caused her trouble. She inched the tractor forward, then backward, then forward again. After each move, she had to climb down from the cab to see if she could slip the heavy metal pin through the hitch and tractor drawbar. Five times she climbed down, until she finally got it right. She dropped the pin in place and connected the eight hydraulic hoses. She climbed back aboard and touched the hydraulic control to raise the huge piece of equipment off the ground and onto its wheels, then collapsed the two outer wings inward so she could maneuver the thing through the gate. She was ready. She stopped for another fifteen seconds to adjust the stereo to her liking, and she was off.

She eased the big tractor slowly out of the yard onto the road, the weight of the disk behind bouncing the front of the tractor just enough to give her a queasy feeling in the pit of her stomach. She slipped into a higher gear and roared up the road to the gate. Out of the corner of her eye, she could see Sugar trailing along behind. She smiled. *A good omen for my first day,* she thought. *Sugar has given her approval.* She slowed, made a wide turn, and then slowed still more, this time to a crawl as she fit the wide disk through the open gate. She looked behind her from one side to the other, one foot on the clutch and the other on the brake. The clearance for what she had on behind was more than a foot on each side, but it seemed far less to her. She was through. So far so good. She turned left and made her way the hundred yards or so to the fence marking the edge of the field. She glanced behind her out the glassed-in cab and was surprised to see the deep tire tracks she was making. I forgot how much this thing weighs, she thought. But still, there was no cause for alarm. The tractor was moving easily over the broken cornstalks.

She spun the steering wheel as she neared the fence, turning to head the tractor down the long length of the field. She stopped to extend the wings of the disk and then gauged carefully to make sure she was far enough from the fence. *All I need is to get the end of this thing caught in the fence,* she thought to herself. She looked about her to make sure Sugar was well out of the way, but the black and white spaniel was already a quarter mile ahead, checking the tall weeds by the fence for a rabbit to chase. "Well, here goes nothing," Katie said aloud as she let out the clutch, eased the throttle forward, and nudged the lever that dropped the disk into the ground.

The tractor belched black smoke under the sudden load, and its roar deepened as the shiny disks dug into the soil, swirling the cornstalks, roots and all, into a blend. She could see great clods of dirt flying from each wheel, and suddenly she noticed she wasn't moving. She pushed the throttle still further forward. The tractor roared, and the two big wheels spun wildly in place as they dug two giant holes with their spinning. Katie jammed her foot in on the clutch, and the wheels stopped. She uttered a string of well-chosen words. "Now I've gone and done it." She clicked off the stereo, which wasn't doing a thing for her mood at the moment, and climbed down to the ground. She walked slowly around the tractor. It was hard to see treads on the two big tires, they were so clotted with mud. The holes they had dug were two feet deep, and she could see the yellow clay they had unearthed. *Hmm, maybe Gram was right,* she thought to herself. She walked behind the disk. It was mired in the sticky mud.

Katie climbed back into the cab. Her heart was hammering like she had just run a mile. *Take it easy now. This isn't the end of the world. We'll get out of this.* She hit the hydraulic lever and lifted the disk out of the ground. "Now, let's see what we can do," she said aloud. She put the tractor in gear and pushed the throttle forward. The rear wheels only dug deeper. She shoved in the clutch again and throttled back. She sat rubbing her chin, listening to the low roar of the tractor. The frown on her face suddenly changed to a smile. "I've got it! Let's get rid of some weight." She used the hydraulic control to drop the disk back onto the ground, climbed down again, and began struggling with the hitch. It took her five minutes tugging and twisting to unhitch the disk from the tractor, but finally she got the job done.

When she came back around the side of the tractor to the steps, her boots were so caked with mud she could hardly lift her feet. She peeled one of her muddy gloves off and beat it against the first metal step, then did the same with the other. She struggled back up the steps to the cab. She put the tractor in gear and poured on the gas. The rear wheels spun in their trenches but wouldn't climb out. She angrily stomped on the clutch. *What am I going to do?* Her eyebrows knitted in worry as she sat in the big seat, thinking. She slipped the tractor back in gear and tried gently rocking from reverse to forward, but that didn't work. She tried easing the tractor slowly to climb out of the holes, but the wheels couldn't get any traction. She tried again at full throttle, more out of frustration than anything, but the tractor only dug deeper. *I've really done it now,* she thought as she throttled back.

She climbed down again wearily and slogged slowly

around the front of the tractor. That's when she saw David's truck go by, slow at the gate, and pull in. "Damn!" she shouted over the rhythmic roar of the tractor. "Why does he always catch me at times like this?" She watched as he walked slowly toward her.

"Having a little trouble?" he asked when he got close enough to be heard. She could see the beginning of a smile on his face.

She stood with her hands on her hips, mud-splattered, red-faced, her boots all but unidentifiable as boots, red hair sticking out on all sides of her University of Illinois cap. "David Cairn, if you don't wipe that smile off your face, I'll, I'll . . ." She couldn't think of a fitting end to her threat, but he got the picture.

"Simmer down. It's not as bad as all that. You should be able to drive it right out by, oh, I'd say July." He laughed out loud.

Katie tried to stamp her foot, but she had trouble lifting her muddy boot. "Did you hear me? This is not a laughing matter!"

He walked over to the tractor and looked into one of the trenches dug by a wheel. "What were you trying to do anyway?"

"What do you think I was trying to do? Disk. What does it look like?"

He was still staring into one of the muddy holes. "Well, to be honest, it looks like you were trying to dig a well." He turned toward her and grinned.

"That's it. Go! Get off my land this instant! If all you can do is stand around making smart remarks, then leave."

"Hey, take it easy. I'm sorry. But don't you know it's too early for you to be out here? The frost is just leaving the ground. That's why it's so muddy."

"Oh, really," she said sarcastically. "Tell me something I don't already know. Like how to get out of here."

He glanced at the disk and made a superhuman effort to be serious. "You've tried unhooking the disk?"

"Yes."

He squinted over at her. "And that didn't help at all?"

"Does it look like it?"

"Did you try rocking it?" he asked, bending down to feel inside the trench.

"Yes."

He looked up. "Not too much, I hope. You can mess up the transmission that way."

"I don't think so," she said, with a touch of concern in her voice. Bad enough she had to worry about getting unstuck. Now he made her wonder if she had ruined the tractor.

He walked around the front of the tractor, went about ten feet ahead, and pawed at the ground with his boot. He strolled slowly back to where she was standing. "I thought so."

"What?"

"There's a real low spot in this corner. Your dad used to have trouble with corn drowning right about here during wet summers. Could be a broken tile. You're right in the middle of it."

"Oh, great!"

"Not to worry. I think if I get my tractor a little ahead of you there, I can pull you out. Want to try it?"

"Might as well. I've tried everything else."

"Okay. I'll be back in twenty minutes." He started walking toward his truck, then turned suddenly. "Hey, now, don't go anywhere," he said, and this time his laugh was loud and long.

As he started to turn back, Katie, blind with fury, reached down in one motion, grabbed a clod of mud tossed up by one of the wheels, and hurled it as hard as she could at him. He saw it coming and tried to duck out of the way, but tripped over a cornstalk, and began to fall. She watched the flight of the clod as if it were in slow motion. She had plenty of time to wonder why she had done such a stupid thing as the clump of dirt homed in on its target like a guided missile. It hit him smack in the back of the head.

He was already falling when the clod hit, and he went down on all fours between two rows of corn stubble. "David!" she screamed. When he heard the scream, he let himself drop the rest of the way to the ground in spite of the mud. He closed his eyes and lay as still as death.

Katie stumbled toward him. "I'm sorry, I'm sorry. I didn't mean to hurt you." She dropped to her knees and grabbed him by the shoulder, shaking gently. "Are you all right?" Her voice was agony. He held himself motionless. "What have I done?" She pulled him over on his back. "I'm so sorry. Please wake up."

He opened one eye. "Did I hear you say you're sorry?" he asked as a smile spread across his muddy face.

Katie stared. Two quite different emotions raced through her. First, total relief, followed close behind by total rage. The rage got the upper hand. "You beast!" she shouted. She took a wild swing and would have hit him square in the face with a fist clenched tightly inside a muddy glove if he hadn't grabbed her wrist.

"You little wildcat!"

"You'll think wildcat!" She shoved her other hand complete with its glop into his face and twisted.

"Why you . . ." He let go of her wrist and grabbed for a handful of soft mud himself, pushing it toward her face. She dodged and the mud caught her on the neck and ear. She reached for her own handful, and he rolled over her to grab the arm with its intended load. She pushed him off, and they rolled together over two rows of corn stubble.

Suddenly he loosed his grip, laughed out loud, and dropped flat on his back. He grinned up at her, his teeth sparkling white against the mud on his face and his eyes bright with laughter. She stopped struggling, stared at him in surprise, and then laughed herself at how ridiculous they both must look. She looked irresistible to him at that moment, her flaming hair matted, her face splattered with mud, a glob of the stuff sticking to her neck. He reached for her, pulled her to him, and found her lips with his own. Her eyes flew wide in surprise and then closed as she wrapped her arms tight around him to draw him still closer. She could taste the dirt, feel the grit on his lips as she eagerly sought for more. She was all alone with him then, the only sound the rhythmic roar of the tractor throbbing in her ears, or was it her own heart pulsing her blood through her body, making her feel more alive than she had ever felt?

David felt something wet touch his ear, and his eyes snapped open. He pulled away. "What the—?"

"What's the matter?" Katie gasped.

Sugar stood smiling at them, wagging her tail.

"It's only Sugar," she laughed, glad for something to break the tension she was feeling at the moment. "Yeah, Sugar," she said cradling the shaggy head. "You were just saving me from that big, bad man, weren't you, girl?"

David struggled to his feet and held out a hand to pull Katie up. Both busied themselves brushing the mud from their clothes. They were trying desperately to ignore what had just happened. "Don't believe a word, Sugar. She started it."

"Uh-uh," Katie protested.

"The heck you didn't. Trying to kill me with a dirt clod. Where'd you learn to throw like that?" he asked, rubbing the back of his head.

"Softball. How about you? Where did you learn to play dead like that?"

All she got for an answer was a grin. "We'd better get this tractor out," he said. He started to walk backwards in the direction of his pickup. "I'm going to keep an eye on you this time."

Watching him walk away, Katie shook her head. *Did*

what I think happen, really happen? she wondered to herself. She arched her eyebrows. *Oh, it happened all right. I can't believe we were actually rolling around on the ground.* She glanced toward the road. *Gee, what if somebody had come along just then? They would have gotten an eyeful.*

An hour later, Katie clomped onto the front porch and balanced on each foot as she struggled with her muddy shoestrings. She dumped the boots on the floor, doubting she would ever be able to get them clean again. She made her way into the house. Gram, busy with lunch, shouted out to her from the kitchen, "How's your first day going?"

"Not so very good," Katie answered.

Gram came to the doorway. "Why? What went . . . ?" She brought her hand to her mouth. "What in the world happened to you? You're mud from head to toe."

Katie grinned. "And you haven't even seen my boots."

"Did you fall?"

"Hmm," Katie began thoughtfully. "I guess you could say that." She recovered herself. "No, I didn't fall—exactly. You can't believe how muddy it was out there. You were right. I had no business going out today. I got stuck. Oh, did I ever get stuck. It was a big mess. You just wouldn't believe it. Luckily, David came along to help."

Gram was watching Katie with a questioning look on her face. "You seem mighty pleased with yourself, considering the looks of you." Her eyes widened as Katie turned to drop her muddy gloves by the door. She had to catch herself from laughing out loud. "So you say David helped? That was nice of him." She was grinning as she turned to go back into the kitchen. "Lunch will be ready by the time you get cleaned up. You can tell me all about your exciting morning. I want to hear everything now. Don't leave out a single detail."

Now why is she acting so weird? Katie wondered. She

peeled off her denim jacket and tossed it on the floor by the gloves. She knew she would have to wash all her clothes. Suddenly, she snatched the jacket off the floor and held it up. Two perfect muddy handprints decorated the back.

Chapter Thirteen

Katie didn't tell her grandmother the whole truth. She certainly didn't lie. She just left out huge parts. There was plenty of story to tell anyway—about getting stuck and how bad it was and what she tried on her own to free the tractor and about how David just happened along and then went after his tractor to pull her. Gram was a great listener as usual. She was all properly shocked and worried and relieved at the right times, but Katie knew she was on to something. She had that smirky little smile she could get at times and just drive you crazy with it.

Katie put the whole thing out of her mind as best she could for the rest of the day. She tried to clean the tractor, which was a mess. Then she took the pickup and went back to the field with a shovel. She wanted to fill the two big ruts the tractor tires had made. She had to admit, it was a matter of simple pride. She didn't want neighbors to drive by and figure out that she had been out too early. But the chore didn't go well. It was just too muddy to shovel. She would have to wait a day or two.

Katie waited till that night when she went to bed to finally think through clearly what had happened that morning. *He started the whole thing, didn't he?* she thought to herself. *Well, not the clod business, of course. That was my doing. But he grabbed me. I've got the jacket to prove it. Come to think of it, I'm not going to wash that jacket. And he* kissed *me. But I'm pretty sure we got the idea at the same time. That was funny, the way it just happened so fast. I definitely kissed him back, though.* She grinned up at the ceiling. *He's no slouch in the kissing department. That's the most romantic kiss I've ever had. And in a cornfield? Do you suppose that's ever been done before? How romantic!* For some strange reason she remembered Burt Lancaster and Deborah Kerr on the beach in the old film, *From Here to Eternity. Oh, gee, did we look like the two of them? In a cornfield!*

She propped her hands behind her head. *Now what? What happens next? Does he still think there's something between me and Steve? What can I do about it if he does? I can't very well walk up to him and say, "Oh, by the way, that Steve Prescott you met, he's toast as far as I'm concerned." Anyway, it's possible what happened today may not mean anything to him.* She licked her lips. *It's possible, but I find that highly doubtful. I know what the trouble is. That ex-wife of his has got him all messed up.* She grinned wide again. *Well, I guess she didn't make a complete woman-hater out of him, anyway. No siree! So, what do I do now? It's got to be up to him. I can't hit him on the head and drag him to my cave.* She giggled out loud. *Come to think of it, I've already tried that!*

Katie bounded out of bed the next morning with enough energy to take on the world. She was convinced that what had happened yesterday was going to become the defining moment of the rest of her life. She was as expectant and as hopeful as a six-year-old on Christmas Eve. She thought she and David were ready to pick up where they had left off before Valentine's Day, before that horrible misunderstanding about Steve Prescott. But nothing happened that day, or in the days that followed. He didn't stop by, he didn't call.

A full week passed. Seven days of waiting. Katie became more convinced with each day that David was avoiding her. She knew that she should have at least *seen* him during that time. After all, they lived only a half mile apart. Then one day she and Gram were coming from town and met him on the road as they slowed for the driveway. Katie waited for him to pass before she turned in. They were mere feet apart as his truck went by her car, and she could see his face clearly. He smiled stiffly and waved. Just a friendly "howdy" type of neighborly wave. She did a slow burn as she pulled into the drive. *It would have been better if he'd completely ignored me, driven right on by without so much as looking at me. Well, maybe that isn't exactly true,* she thought. *But a smile and a wave? Come on, who needs that? I don't want to be just friends. Anyway, that was more than a friendly kiss or my name isn't Katherine Ann Rourke. Am I reading too much into a kiss?* she wondered. *Could a first kiss mean as much as I thought that one did? I guess not, but you sure could have fooled me.*

If she had known what he was thinking at that moment on the road or for that matter if she could have somehow seen the turmoil in his head over the last seven days, she might have taken heart, but, of course, she had no such clairvoyant powers.

And just what was going on in that head of his? His first thought, the one that hit him square between the eyes that day in the cornfield was to tell Katie the truth—that he hadn't been able to get her out of his mind since the first night when she walked into the kitchen. So why didn't he tell her? After all, he was pretty sure the kiss was special to her too. He knew one thing—she sure kissed back. What was the matter with him? Why was he such an idiot, acting like a junior-high geek? *What was I supposed to do?* he asked himself later. *We were standing out there in the middle of a field in broad daylight, freezing, covered with mud, with a tractor roaring fifteen feet away. Not much of a place for endearments.*

So, missing that all-important follow-up moment, time became his biggest enemy. Because no sooner was he away from Katie than the doubts began. Did he really love her? It had been so long since he had felt love, he honestly wasn't sure. He hardly knew her, really, he argued with himself. Was he in love with her or was he in love with an ideal, someone who was ready to take on the world no matter what? Maybe she appealed so to him because she was the complete opposite of his ex-wife. But isn't the object of love supposed to be an ideal? he wondered. He just didn't know. One thing he was sure of: his failed marriage was getting in the way. He was afraid of making another mistake. He didn't think he could go through that again. And anyway, what about this fellow from Illinois? How did he fit into the picture?

He was thinking too much for his own good. He picked up the phone three times to call that first day, and each time put the receiver back in the cradle before he could dial. *What is wrong with me? What am I afraid of?* And each day that he waited made it just that much more difficult for him to make that call. And by the third day, he had convinced himself that he had probably taken advantage of Katie, that she was probably disgusted by what had happened, and that, at the very least, she thought he was a stupid fool. All good enough reasons for him to keep his distance.

Katie didn't have much time to brood on lost expectations. She was suddenly too busy. She made an interesting discovery about one big difference between her old profession, teaching, and her new one, farming. Teaching, at least while she was in the middle of doing it each day, always filled up every corner of her mind. There wasn't room for anything else. But the actual doing of farming was something quite different. She discovered long periods of solitude working in the cab of the tractor. She found she could separate parts of her mind somehow. Part of her took care of running the tractor while the other part was free to roam. And that wasn't a good thing right now. Especially when her thoughts were as confusing and unsatisfying as they had been lately.

She worked her ground carefully. This was the easy part, she knew; the harder part would come later, with the planting. But she was becoming more comfortable each day. She learned to handle the tractor, if not expertly then at least adequately, even with the disk or plow or field cultivator on behind. She worried constantly about breakdowns, because when something broke, she felt lost. Many farmers—and her dad had been one of the best of them—could make most repairs themselves. There was a welder in the machine shed, but she hadn't the foggiest idea of how to use it. One day she hit a buried rock and broke a piece off the chisel plow. She was stopped dead for two precious days until the local welder could work her in. And the charge for the repair wasn't cheap for someone on a tight budget. She decided to look into a welding course during the off-season. That ought to raise the hackles of a few men, she decided.

David stayed away, and Gram finally wondered aloud about it one day at dinner. "What in the world is wrong with David Cairn? I thought you two patched things up at the wedding? But here it's been weeks, and we haven't seen hide nor hair of him."

Katie tensed at the mention of David's name, but tried her best to sound offhand. "Oh, I suppose he must be busy. Like everyone this time of year."

"Nonsense. Nobody's so busy they can't stop in for a cup of coffee. If I didn't know better, I'd say he was avoiding us." She looked closely at Katie across the table. "Do you know something you're not telling? You two haven't been at each other again, have you?"

Katie nearly choked at her grandmother's strange choice of words. Maybe it was time to tell Gram what had happened. She was getting tired of keeping it all inside. She took a deep breath and plunged in. "Well, as a matter of fact, you're half right. He's trying to avoid me, not us."

Gram frowned. "Uh-huh. I thought something funny was going on. So what happened now?"

"It's very confusing. You remember that day three weeks ago when I got the tractor stuck and David pulled me out?"

Gram nodded. What she was still remembering were the handprints on Katie's jacket.

"Well, something happened that day between us." She hesitated. "I can't believe I'm telling all this to you. We started out fighting because I was in such a state over the tractor, and he was laughing about it. That sounds like an old story, doesn't it?" Gram nodded. "But then the strangest thing happened. We . . . well, we kissed. Just out of the blue. I know it seems weird, I mean out there in the mud and all, and for the life of me I don't really know how it happened." She let out a long sigh just remembering it. "But Gram, it was wonderful."

Gram studied her granddaughter. She didn't know what to make of this latest story. "You mean the two of you kissed out there in the field where anyone going by on the road could see you?"

"Well, yes, what's so bad about that?"

"Katie, what would the neighbors think?"

"Oh, who cares about the neighbors? We didn't do anything wrong. We kissed, that's all. Now do you want to hear the rest or not?"

Gram folded her hands in her lap. She had a resigned look on her face. "Go on."

Katie laughed a little embarrassed laugh then, and ran her fingers through her hair. "Well, actually, come to think of it, that's about all there is to tell. Then David got his tractor and pulled me out and that was that."

Gram's look changed to a questioning one. "What do you mean that's all? How does that explain why he stopped coming by? Why, after your grandfather kissed me the first time, he made a regular pest of himself at our house.''

"Exactly,'' Katie blurted. Finally, someone who thought David's reaction was strange too. ''That's what I don't understand either. I thought we were about to start something, but it all stopped before it started. Gram, do you think I scared him off or what? I didn't mean to.''

"Hmm.'' Gram rubbed her chin. ''I don't think it has anything to do with you. If you ask me, I expect it's that first wife of his. I told you she was bad business, but you didn't believe me. She's made him afraid of women.'' Gram smiled at Katie and reached over to squeeze her hand. ''You really like him, don't you, dear?''

Katie nodded. ''I do. I've always liked him. I've never told you this, but I had a massive crush on him a long time ago, when I was in grade school even.'' She reddened slightly. She had never told a soul about that. ''And when I came into the kitchen that first night and saw him at the table, I could have died.'' She shook her head. ''But he hasn't said so much as a word since that day in the mud. I know he's avoiding me. I see him, but he's so far away, all we do is wave. Just like neighbors. Like I wave at Ron Hemmingford when he drives by, or even old Otto Struebler. I mean, I know we're neighbors, but I don't want to be just his friend. Am I making any sense at all?''

"Of course you are. But don't worry, he'll come to his senses soon enough.'' She narrowed her eyes in thought. *That dear boy is worse off than I thought. He's going to need a shove, and I'm just the one to give it to him.*

And it didn't take her long to get started. She needed help, though. She called Becky to come for coffee that very afternoon. While Lena played blocks on the kitchen floor, Gram started her prying, knowing that Katie was on the tractor in a field somewhere and couldn't shush her or act shocked or show her disapproval in some other way. *Hon-*

estly, I don't understand young people these days, she thought to herself. *How are they ever going to find out things if they don't ask?* She freshened Becky's coffee. Most of the usual gossip had already been dispensed with, so Gram asked, all innocence, "Have you seen David lately?"

Becky leaned forward. "Funny you mention him. Otis is terrible worried about him, you know. Says he's been actin' mighty unlike himself."

Gram perked up. "Oh? What do you mean?"

"Well, he's been in just the worst mood lately. Why, just the day before yesterday Otis asked him all plain and simple whether he'd seen you folks of late. You know Otis, he didn't mean nothing by it. Well, Dave like to bit his head off. Said how was he supposed to know. Now, you know, that's just not like him."

Gram showed her surprise. "Well, I should say it isn't."

"Like I said to Otis, it's a shame to see such a nice person so down on himself. He's been awful good to us, you know. Why, Otis is like a different person now he's here in Willow Grove. It just sorely pains the both of us to see Dave this way. Otis thinks it's got somethin' to do with that ex-wife of his. Did you know her?"

"To be plain about it, no one around here really knew her," Gram answered. "She was what you might call a little uppity, if you know what I mean."

"How long were they married?"

"No more than a couple of years. She's a lawyer. Worked in Des Moines, so we didn't see much of her. And neither did he, I'd bet you."

Becky reached down to push a block toward Lena. "Too bad he can't find somebody else. I was kinda hopin' it might be Katie. Did you watch them two at the wedding? Otis and me sure did. Why, they was looking at each other every chance they got, and not just at the wedding either.

We been remarking on it right along. Surely you must a noticed too?''

"Well, now that you bring it up, I declare I have seen some looks going back and forth between the two of them.''

"See there? It's not just us then. Otis even said something to Dave a while back, but he said we must a been imaginin' things.''

"Is that a fact?'' Gram nodded her head thoughtfully. She'd had confederates all along, and she hadn't even known it.

Chapter Fourteen

Esther Pitcher hadn't driven a car since her surgery a little over three years ago. She had long ago gotten over her frustration at the inconvenience, but she was feeling it now. She needed to talk to David Cairn—alone—and was having trouble figuring out just how to do it, since she couldn't go looking for him. She thought about inviting him for a meal, but that just wouldn't do. She didn't think bringing the two together right now was a good thing. Not until she did a little groundwork. It was a little past seven. Katie had gobbled her supper and headed back out to finish disking a field, much against Gram's protests. Gram didn't like this night work and absolutely put her foot down about fieldwork after dark. So far Katie had obeyed, and was always safely in the house before dark.

Mrs. Pitcher picked up the phone and dialed. As the phone rang, she hoped that David hadn't gone back to the field too. But he was at home, and she was ready with an offer he couldn't refuse. She had made a lemon meringue pie that very afternoon, and thought he might like some of it. She was taking definite advantage, because she happened to know that lemon meringue was his favorite. He was in the yard in five minutes. She smiled to herself as he walked up onto the front porch.

"Well, let me look at you," she welcomed him. "Why, I thought you dropped off the face of the earth. Where *have* you been?"

He grinned sheepishly. "I guess it has been a while. I've been keeping busy. We're just about ready to start planting."

"You don't need to tell me. Katie has been working herself silly." She shook her head. "I hope she knows what she's doing. You'll have a cup of coffee, won't you? And a small slice of pie? To see if it's worth taking home? We had some for supper, and I thought it was a might tart." She set a generous slice in front of him.

"Mrs. P, you always say that." He took a bite, savoring it. "And it's delicious, as always." He looked up at her as she was pouring coffee. "Where's Katie anyway?"

"Out in the field. See what I'm telling you? She's working her fingers to the bone." She sat with her own cup of coffee and stole a quick glance over at him. "I'm worried about her, you know. She doesn't look well. Her eyes, you know. They're just sunken into her head. She's not eating enough to keep a bird alive. And I don't think she's been sleeping. She gets up with the chickens and works into the night." She took a sip of coffee and decided to stop there, before she went too far.

David frowned. He knew he shouldn't have stayed away. "Is she behind with the fieldwork?"

Gram was pretty sure Katie had things well in hand, but she crossed her fingers under the table before she answered. "I don't know for sure. She never likes to worry me, you know, but I think she might be getting behind. Else why would she be out there right now?"

David nodded gravely. "I was afraid this might happen. That's a lot of land for one person, especially someone who's new to it all. I'll stop by and see her on my way home or tomorrow if I can't catch her tonight. Otis and I can pitch in if she's behind."

Gram smiled. "That would be so good of you boys. I knew I could count on you."

David took a sip of coffee and cleared his throat. "Uh,

maybe that Prescott fellow can lend a hand as soon as school is out.'' He was stretching to get information.

Gram's eyes gleamed. This was more than she could have hoped for. She had been worried about how to bring Steve into the conversation. ''Oh, him, no, no, that's all over. Well, not that there was anything between them anyway. He was just a friend.''

David's eyes brightened. ''He seemed more than just a friend to me.''

''No, no. Well, he may have thought he was more than a friend, but Katie never did. In fact, she sent him packing not more than fifteen minutes after you left that day you met him.''

''She did?'' He was surprised, and obviously delighted with this news.

''Oh, my yes.'' Gram was pouring it on. ''You probably didn't know it, but Katie was very upset with him for driving all the way out here for no good reason.'' She watched David's reaction with pleasure. ''No, I think we've seen the last of him. Nice boy, but not Katie's type.''

David had a satisfied smile on his face. ''That's very interesting.'' He looked at his watch. ''I was hoping she'd get home before I left, but I've got to check my cattle before dark.'' He pushed his chair back. ''I'll look in on her tomorrow, so don't you worry, Mrs. P.'' He took the container of pie she offered. ''Thanks much for the pie. Sorry I've been ignoring you two. I'll be stopping by more often now that we're caught up with the fieldwork.''

I just bet you will, she said to herself as she fought to keep from smiling. She wagged a finger at him. ''Well, I should hope so. We're just two helpless women living here, you know.'' She felt guilty about her manipulation of him for about as long as it took him to drive out of the yard.

The next day was warm and breezy. David and Otis were carrying bags of seed corn to the pickup from a shed where it had been stored. When they finished, David checked his watch. "Why don't you take the planter up to your place, and I'll meet you there with the seed? You want to start the planting, or should I?"

"Well," Otis drawled, "I'm up to tryin' it if you ain't got nothin' against crooked rows."

"You'll do just fine. After I get you started, I'm coming back here and get that eighty acres ready."

"Okay by me. Say, afore I forget it, Becky said for you to stop for noon dinner. She's fixin' fried chicken, and there'll be plenty."

David nervously adjusted his cap. "I can't keep imposing on you folks. That's three times this week."

"Ain't no trouble, I'm tellin' ya. Least we can do, anyways."

"Fried chicken, you say?"

Otis grinned. "That's right. And plenty of it, don't forget."

"Well, okay, you twisted my arm." He opened the door to the truck. "I've got a little errand to take care of. I might be a few minutes." He climbed in and Otis headed for the tractor, glad to see his boss in a better frame of mind.

David could see where Katie was working because of the cloud of dust following her tractor. He pulled through the gate and stopped at the edge of the field. She was three hundred yards away, but coming toward him. He strained his eyes to make out her form riding confidently in the big cab. She reached the end, made a neat turn, and aimed back in the other direction before she stopped and throttled back. He marveled at how well she handled the tractor. She pushed open the door and climbed down the steps. He watched her as she walked toward him. She was wearing jeans and a bright red pullover shirt. She had on her U of I baseball cap and as usual her red hair stuck out all around. She smiled somewhat uncertainly as she came near him.

She had practically given up wondering why he had stopped coming around. He noticed how white her teeth showed against the browning skin of her face. Her arms, too, were beginning to tan, even though it was only May. Looking at her, he couldn't help but remember the kiss, and he cursed himself silently for staying away. He vowed to change all that. Remembering Mrs. Pitcher's worry, he studied her as she came closer. *She looks great to me,* he thought, *but Mrs. P must know what she's talking about.*

The two nodded awkwardly to each other. The sudden intimacy of their last meeting was making it difficult to know how to proceed. "What's up?" she asked, watching him curiously.

"Not much. I just wanted to see how you're doing." He studied her eyes carefully, but for the life of him couldn't see that they looked sunken.

"I'm just fine." Her smile faded a little under his scrutiny.

Never one for small talk, he jumped awkwardly right into the middle of things. "Listen, Otis and I can slip over and get you caught up in two days. It wouldn't be any problem at all."

Now the smile was gone entirely from her face *and* her voice. "What are you talking about, anyway? I don't need anyone to 'slip over.' I'm doing just fine here, thank you."

"Now, don't get all worked up. I know you want to do it all by yourself, but there's no shame in accepting a little help from a neighbor," he blundered on. "I mean, it's the first time you've done all this. And you being a woman and all." *Uh-oh! I've done it again,* he realized too late. *Watch out for flying dirt clods.*

And he was right, of course. Katie's flaming red hair would have been standing on end, except for the baseball cap. "What does my being a woman have to do with it?" she snapped.

He held both hands out in front of him. "Stop. Please,

spare me the lecture. I've heard it all before. I know, I know, it's the woman thing. You *are* a woman. So is it my fault if I happen to notice that every time I see you? All I wanted to do was offer help if you need it. And it's obvious you're too blasted stubborn to admit when you need help.''

This was too much. Katie stamped her foot so hard a small cloud of dust puffed up around her boot. ''I've never seen such arrogance. You think because I'm a woman, I must need help.''

''I didn't say that.''

''No, but you were thinking it. You've been thinking it from the very beginning. Well, for your information, I don't need help. I'm working my last field, and I'm ready to start planting tomorrow. So there!''

''You are impossible! I wouldn't help you now even if you begged me.'' He spun on his heel and stomped back to the pickup. She climbed back into her tractor, and they went off in opposite directions.

It didn't take Gram long at noon dinner to figure out she had really botched things this time, maybe beyond repair. She was afraid for the dishes, the way Katie was knocking things about. When she heard what he had said, all she could do was shake her head. That man is hopeless, she thought to herself. But she had to say something. After all, she was responsible.

''Dear, I think I might have had a little part in all this.''

Katie eyed her grandmother. ''What do you mean?''

''I might have given David the idea you could use a little help.''

Now Katie glared. ''Gram, how could you?''

''I'm sorry. I really am. I was just trying to push him a little. How was I to know he'd put his foot in it like he did?''

Katie threw her hands in the air. ''Well, that's the end

of that. We won't be seeing David Cairn around here any-time soon.''

Gram sat at the end of the table, her head down, looking as if she could burst into tears at any moment. ''I know, I'm just a silly old lady who keeps getting in everyone's way.''

Katie jumped from her chair and wrapped her arms around her grandmother. ''That's not true. You're the dear-est person in the world. It's just that sometimes you say things before you think them through. Now promise me you won't meddle like this again.''

''I promise,'' she said solemnly, but her hands were rest-ing on her lap under her napkin, the fingers crossed. She was already thinking of what she could do to make up for the mess she had caused.

And things didn't go much better at the Skibbys'. Unlike Gram, who as the cause of this latest trouble, at least knew what it was all about, Otis and Becky were clueless. David wasn't talking, period. Well, that wasn't exactly true. They did get a yes or no out of him two or three times, and ''Uncle'' Dave was his usual sweet self to little Lena. But she was the only one he seemed to notice. All in all, it was one very long, uncomfortable meal with a dinner guest whose thoughts were a million miles away.

Chapter Fifteen

Katie had little time to reflect on this latest fiasco in her relationship with David Cairn. She was engaged in the biggest challenge of her short farming career—getting the corn planted. When she went to the first field the next day with the big planter behind the tractor, she knew it was the start of a battle, a battle with time and the weather. The window of opportunity for getting the seed in the ground was a narrow one. Katie pulled to the edge of the field by the fence. She gauged the distance from the fence to her planter. She eased the tractor into gear and started across the field at a steady speed. She knew this first pass was the key to straight rows. A marker arm extending from the right of the planter was etching a shallow trench in the dirt that she would follow with her tractor wheels on the return trip. And she would repeat that process, following that marked trail back and forth until she reached the fence at the other side. But there was nothing to follow on the first trip except the fence.

She'd been worried about planting for weeks. She knew it was silly. Straight rows, crooked rows—it really didn't make that much difference. But she knew farmers judged each other by just such a highly visible standard. She remembered her dad poking along in the pickup appraising neighbors' fields and pointing out the occasional one that looked like it had been planted by the light of a waning moon. It was a matter of pride. And she was under extra pressure. Every farmer from miles around would drive slowly by her fields when the corn first appeared, fully expecting to see crooked rows. Well, they'd be disappointed, or she'd know the reason why.

She'd been practicing. While she disked or plowed or used the field cultivator, she worked hard at keeping the tractor going straight across the field. And she'd gotten pretty good at it. Now she was nearing the end. She stopped. Before she turned the tractor and planter to prepare for the return pass, she twisted in her seat and looked back where she had come. It was hard to tell, but the row looked straight to her. She'd know soon enough, when the green shoots pushed their way out of the ground.

It took her eleven hectic days to get her four hundred acres of corn planted. She would have been done earlier, but she'd had trouble with the planter and had to take it to the John Deere dealer in Willow Grove for repairs. That was an experience. The trip in by tractor, trying to stay clear of bridges and cars and traffic signs, with the wide load on behind, was bad enough. But then she had to put up with the smirks and stares from the counterman and his cohorts back in the shop. She managed to control her temper, which would have made her grandmother proud. The shop foreman, a chain-smoking, grease-stained fellow with a self-assured grin that Katie would have gladly volunteered to slap off his face, claimed the problem was a simple adjustment. Katie knew better. She'd tried every adjustment in the book—literally, with the book in her hand. And it turned out she was right. The problem was a broken tooth on a cog, and the laugh was on Eugene—that was the name printed on the front of his green coveralls. Katie sang all the way home.

The planting was monotonous and tiring as well as just plain hard work. Her arms and shoulders ached from lugging bags of seed corn from the truck to the planter. At night she fell into bed before the ten o'clock news and slept like a dead person. She was up with the sun and out in the field again after a quick breakfast. And then the monotony set in. Following the marker with the wheels of her tractor became hypnotizing. She had to shake herself to keep from falling asleep at the wheel, especially when she went out to the field after her noon meal. More than once she climbed down out of the tractor in the middle of the field and did jumping jacks to try to force the sleep from her brain. At times like that, she knew she had good reason to worry about the straightness of her rows.

And then she was done. She finished on a Thursday— late. She had gone out after supper because the forecast was for rain, and she wanted to finish before the rains came. She had been living a charmed life as far as the weather was concerned. The only rain while she was planting had come during the night before she took the planter in for repairs. The rain probably would have kept her out of the field that day anyway, so she felt she really didn't lose any time for the breakdown.

She pulled to the end of the last round in the last field about eight o'clock. The sun was sinking fast. Katie felt such exhilaration, she didn't know what to do with herself. It was like the last day of school, only better. She leaned back in the tractor seat and surveyed the field in front of her. *I've accomplished so much,* she thought. *I showed them. But I'd better not get carried away,* she reminded herself. *I've still got a long way to go. But, what the heck, I've got a right to be proud.* She mentally ticked off what had got her this far. *I learned how to run the machinery, I got all the fields worked, and I got the corn in the ground. And I'm done! And I did it all myself!*

She climbed down from the tractor and plopped herself on the ground in the middle of the markings of two rows of corn, just to watch the sunset. Here she was practically living with nature, and she'd been too busy to notice. She could make out the cluster of trees where her own house stood. As her eyes scanned the familiar countryside of her childhood, the sun dropped to the horizon, outlining, as if for her alone, the gentle rises and falls of the patchwork fields with such a golden color it took her breath away. She dug her two hands deep into the loose, rich soil at her sides and let the dirt sift through her fingers. "I've done my part," she said aloud, "now it's your turn." She had yet to learn that the mother of all growing things didn't always listen.

Chapter Sixteen

That night, late, a gentle rain spread over the heartland of Iowa. Katie awoke about two-thirty to a steady drumming on the eaves outside her south window, and she crawled out of bed to see if her curtains were getting wet. Satisfied they weren't, she climbed back under the covers and savored the sound and fresh smell of the rain. The timing couldn't have been more perfect for her. She hugged her pillow. One worry down, now for the next one—what to do about David. She'd been agonizing over that for the last eleven days, but for the life of her, she didn't know what to do. Knowing Gram's part in the whole business, she understood he wasn't entirely to blame. But that still didn't excuse him for the things he'd said.

Not more than half a mile away, David Cairn was awake, staring at the ceiling and listening to the same sounds. He was not happy. He and Otis were behind. They still had two hundred fifty acres to plant in corn yet, and not all of that ground had even been worked. He couldn't remember such a spring for trouble, all of it mechanical. First a tractor, then a plow, and finally the planter. And now this rain. They were certain to lose another two days at least. He wondered how Katie was doing. He had seen her off and on in the field, but after their last encounter, he wasn't going near her. He smiled in the darkness. He had heard the story about her outsmarting Gene at John Deere. Everyone knew about it by now. Things like that got around, and

Gene wasn't any too happy. He'd been putting up with more than his share of ribbing.

It rained all the next day and part of the night. Gently but steadily. Katie checked her rain gauge when it was all over and measured one and a half inches. It had soaked in beautifully though, and she knew the tiny kernels of corn would be fairly bursting to get out of the ground. She started checking her fields for sprouting. Too early, she knew, but she couldn't help herself. She came in almost late for noon dinner.

"Where have you been?" Gram asked. She was putting a hot casserole on the table. "I thought you were all done."

"I am, but . . ."

Gram interrupted. "Don't tell me, you're digging, aren't you? I never saw the like of it. Every farmer's the same. They're always out digging to see if the corn's sprouted. Your own father was the worst of the lot."

"I know, but I can't help it." She was draining the peas in the sink. "That little kernel of corn is down there, and I just have to see if it's starting to grow."

"It'll grow in its own good time. You can't speed things up with all that scratching around." She laid a hand on Katie's shoulder. "It proves one thing though. You're a farmer for sure if you're out digging." She chuckled, but then grew suddenly serious. "I am so proud of you, dear. You said you'd do it and you did."

Katie felt a chill of pride run up her spine. "Thanks, Gram. I couldn't have done it without you, but don't forget we've got a long, long way to go before the corn's in the bin. There're about a hundred things, at least, that can go wrong."

Gram gave Katie's ear a playful twist like she used to do when Katie was a little girl. "Now I'm going to tell you what I always told your father. Don't dig it all up. There won't be anything left to pick in the fall."

* * *

Next day, Katie was out in the pickup cruising her fields. She had to admit Gram was probably right. She was becoming a little obsessed. She couldn't stay away, even though she knew full well no corn shoots would appear for another week. She spotted David across the road, using a field cultivator. *So look who's behind. He doesn't even have all his ground worked.* He was halfway to the end, coming her way, and the gate to his field was right there handy. On the spur of the moment, she suddenly whipped the wheel of the pickup and pulled through the gate into his field. It was time to take action. She had an idea to rattle his cage just a little. If it worked, great. If not, well, things couldn't be much worse between them than they already were.

She climbed out of the pickup as he reached the end. He made his turn and slowed the engine to an idle. She watched him climb down and come toward her.

"Good morning," she said.

He eyed her warily. *What is she up to?* he wondered, remembering all too well their last meeting. "Good morning. You mean you're still talking to me?"

It was obvious his fur was still ruffled—and after nearly two weeks. "About that. We both said things we shouldn't have. Could we just forget it ever happened?"

He was pacified somewhat. He wasn't enjoying the cold war going on between them. "Well, okay by me."

"Good. I just stopped by to ask you something."

He was all seriousness, ready to help. "Sure, shoot."

"I was wondering if you'd like me to whip my tractor over here and help? I'm finished, but it looks like you're a little behind."

It took him a second or two to understand her intention. When he did, he registered surprise. "Hey, that's no fair, throwing my words back at me. I thought you said we were going to forget all that."

She smiled coyly at him. "I lied." Then she doubled

over and slapped her knee. "I'm sorry, I couldn't resist. Are you mad?"

He smiled. "No, I guess you earned bragging rights if you're really done."

He had taken her little ribbing well, and she was pleased. "Well, I'm all done. Finished the night before the rain, thank goodness."

He stuck his hands in his back pockets. "I've got to hand it to you. You left us in the dust. But listen, it would be a different story if it hadn't been for all the breakdowns. And the rain didn't help any, that's for sure."

"Excuses, excuses." Her laugh was carefree.

He shook his head. "I can't believe you're all done! The way your grandmother was going on, I thought you were in trouble."

There it was, out in the open, the reason for their argument. "Gram tends to exaggerate," was all Katie said.

"Oh. Well, say, congratulations on getting your first crop in. I mean it. And you did it all yourself. It doesn't surprise me, though. I knew you could do it."

Katie was glowing. She was surprised at his words. "Thanks. It feels so good."

"Course, I didn't think you'd beat us, but that's all right." He turned to go. "Now you have to hope it comes up." He put on his most serious face. "I sure hope you didn't plant too deep. It'll just rot in the ground, and that's the end of the game."

Katie waved her hands frantically in front of her and made a face. "Don't say things like that."

He aimed a finger at her and laughed. "Gotcha!"

Chapter Seventeen

The one day Katie hadn't checked her fields, of course, the little corn shoots surprised her and peeked out. She and Gram were heading to town for groceries when Gram spotted the new corn first. "I see something," she sang as they drove by the south field.

"What?" Katie slammed on the brakes.

"Right there," Gram chortled. "You can just see the rows. Oh, Katie, they look so straight."

Katie was still staring in shock across her grandmother out the window. "I can't believe it. I swear there wasn't a thing there yesterday afternoon."

"I told you that's the way it would be. You can't rush those little darlings."

"Isn't it beautiful, Gram?" She poked her grandmother's shoulder playfully. "And, of course, you *would* be the first to see it."

Gram beamed. "Well, I've still got my eyes. Might not be good for much else, but I can see like an eagle."

Katie pulled into the field and hopped out to take a closer look. She walked slowly between the rows that were starting to form. Some of the green shoots were pushing toward the sky, while in other spots they hadn't broken through the ground, but Katie could see the cracks in the soil where they were struggling to get out. She heard a car and turned in time to see Otis's rusty Ford pull in behind the pickup.

He and Becky piled out. Becky busied herself with Lena's car seat.

"They're a comin', ain't they?" shouted Otis. He passed Gram's side of the pickup and tipped his cowboy hat. "Mornin', Mrs. P. Beautiful day out." He walked slowly toward Katie in the field. "You done it, little lady. First corn in the neighborhood, by my reckonin'."

Becky came up just then holding Lena, who had her face buried in her mother's shoulder. The sun was too bright for her eyes. "Oh, Katie, aren't you just so proud? You did it! You really did it all by yourself."

Katie beamed. "Thanks, but remember it's early. A lot of things can happen before October." She shaded her eyes and scanned the field, her smile growing. "It does look pretty, doesn't it? I can hardly wait for David to see it." She whirled toward Otis. "He doesn't have anything up yet, does he?"

Becky and Otis exchanged glances. "No, ma'am. Why we just barely got everything in the ground."

Katie took Lena from her mother as they retraced their steps to the gate. "Did you see Aunt Katie's corn?" She held up her hand to shield the baby's face. "Oh, that sun is so bright for little girls, isn't it?"

By the end of the week, Katie could see the corn in all of her fields. In fact, in the first field she'd planted, the one where Gram had first spotted green, the sprouts were so tall, the little leaves even shook in the breeze. She set out Friday afternoon decked out in shorts and a tank top for such a glorious late May day, determined to walk the whole farm. And she did it, too, though she was dragging when she finished, and the bad news was she was a good two miles from home. As far as she could tell, the crop looked perfect. *I'm going to be a nervous wreck by harvest time if I keep this up,* she thought to herself. *I've got to learn to ease up.*

She walked out on the road from her last field and started plodding along the soft shoulder, looking out over the fields as she walked and kicking the occasional rock into the ditch. She was so deep in thought she didn't hear the pickup approach from behind until David pulled up next to her.

"Hey there, need a lift?"

She smiled in at him, glad for the ride. "Don't mind if I do," she said as she opened the door and climbed in.

David accelerated slowly, looking closely at her field. "Say, where did you learn to drive a tractor so straight? Your rows are as perfect as railroad tracks."

She leaned back against the headrest and smiled. "I've been practicing. Besides, you're looking at my best field. I did this one last. Wait till you see my first one."

"The one by the house?"

She nodded.

"Looks fine to me."

She sat up and looked at him in mock reproach. "Why, Mr. Cairn, have you been checking up on me?"

He speeded up and looked ahead at the road. "No, I just happened to be driving by."

"Uh-huh." They rode in silence. "Are you finished planting?" she asked.

"Yep. Finished the day before yesterday. Finally."

"That's good. Now it can rain all it wants. Right?"

"Well, let's keep it reasonable. We don't need a flood."

She suddenly stared down at her arms, which showed a definite tan line between her elbow and her shoulder. "Look at me. I've got a farmer tan started."

He glanced over. "You won't get a farmer tan wearing an outfit like that."

"This is the first day I've worn a tank. Usually I wear a short-sleeve shirt. See the tan up to here? And my legs are hopeless. All pasty white."

He glanced over again, uncomfortably trying not to stare at her legs. "They look okay to me."

Her neck and face reddened. She wasn't really fishing for a compliment on her legs, only making silly conversation, she realized. He turned into the drive and pulled up to the garage. "Thanks a lot," she said as she started to open the door. "I wasn't looking forward to the long walk home."

"No problem." He hurried on before she could leave. "Say, I was wondering . . ."

She stopped with her hand on the door handle.

"Well, you know, since you've got your first crop up and all, and, well, I finally got mine planted, if maybe we could . . . celebrate."

She looked at him. He was struggling to get the words out. She hadn't seen him like this, and it surprised her a little. "Sure, that sounds like fun. What did you have in mind?"

"How about we could go to the Amana Colonies? Make a day of it. Get there for lunch and then bum around in the afternoon, maybe have dinner, and then head back. It's only a little more than an hour's drive."

"Sounds like fun. When? Tomorrow?"

"If that's all right with you."

"Sure. I haven't been there for years and years. All I can remember is the food."

He laughed. "You don't go away hungry, that's for sure."

"So what time?"

"Hmm. How about I pick you up about ten?" His voice sounded more natural now.

"Sounds good. See you then." She opened the door and hopped out. "Bye."

He watched her walk toward the house before he slipped the truck into reverse. *I don't see a darned thing wrong with those legs,* he thought to himself.

Chapter Eighteen

Katie's day with David was perfect. The weather—clear blue sky, seventy-five-degree temperature, no wind—was just right. The seventy-mile drive through the slowly greening patchwork fields began with cautious talk between the two about the simple things they already knew they shared—high school, farming, the town of Willow Grove. But not more than ten miles down the highway, they had already found their comfort zone. Katie was surprised to discover the interests they shared. They both liked science fiction, Asimov especially. They both wanted to learn to fly. Katie had handled the controls on a Piper once and had been hooked. David was dreaming of buying a plane and keeping a small landing strip on the farm. Of course, he would have to take lessons first. He'd been putting that off. They were both sports nuts, especially about basketball. Their baseball allegiance provided a source for some argument, though. He was a Chicago White Sox fan, which didn't set well with her. She had been dreaming of a Cubs World Series for as long as she could remember. Well, nobody's perfect, she decided.

They stopped in the village of Middle Amana first to look for a place to eat. As they left the car, he took her hand to help her across a puddle of water and then didn't let go as they explored the tiny village. Her hand, held tightly in his, felt so right. They found a cozy eating spot, really the dining room of a house that doubled as an antique shop. After lunch they wandered slowly through the other rooms, loaded with warm oak furniture, delicate china, and sparkling crystal. Katie found an unusual thimble for Gram's collection on a table of bric-a-brac. They busied themselves during the afternoon visiting each of the seven colonies. In High Amana they took a winery tour, tasting dandelion, rhubarb, strawberry, and plum before each decided on a bottle to bring home.

They stopped at the museum in Homestead and listened to a gray-haired village woman, dressed in the dark clothing of the early Amana settlers, describe the communal life of the original colonies. They visited the furniture factory and showroom, a working woolen mill, and two more antique shops in the town of Amana, the largest of the colonies. They decided to stay there for dinner because Katie saw the Ox Yoke Inn and remembered it from years before when she had visited with her mom and dad.

They ate too much and definitely didn't need the fresh rhubarb pie to top things off, but it was an outing and they were celebrating, so they indulged. And it was the best rhubarb pie Katie had tasted. If you didn't count Gram's, that is. Then the ride back: They talked easily about the day as two people do when they're no longer worried about saying just the right things. Long moments of silence felt just fine. David pulled into her driveway as the stars were beginning to wink on. Katie had already wished on the very first one miles ago. He walked her to the porch and took both of her hands in his.

"I had fun," she said.

"Me too," David responded. He pulled her close and lightly kissed her lips. "See you." He dropped her hands and walked quickly to the car.

Katie was bewildered by his abruptness. She stood thoughtfully, watching him pull out of the driveway before she went into the house. She slipped into the living room and fell into a chair across from Gram, who was intent over a counted cross-stitch as usual. Gram set her work on the table next to her chair. She could tell Katie wanted to talk. It might have been a sigh or a look or a certain shrug of the shoulders, but she knew.

"So, how was your day?"

"Oh, just fine. But I ate too much. I've never seen so much food, and I had a huge piece of rhubarb pie I didn't need. I'm not going to eat a thing tomorrow."

Gram chuckled. "They do know how to feed folks, I'll give them that." She watched Katie over her glasses. "So what all did you do? I haven't been to the Amanas for years."

"I hadn't either. I think maybe I went with you and grandpa last time." She leaned back. "We saw everything. The furniture store and a winery. Oh, I just remembered, I bought a bottle of dandelion wine for you to try, but I left it in the car."

Gram made a face.

"No, really, it's very good. You'll be surprised. Let's see, what else? We went to two antique shops, well, no, three if you count the one where we ate lunch. Oh, that reminds me." She dug in her purse. "I got you something." She produced the silver thimble.

Gram took it carefully, slipped it on a finger, and held it to the light. "It's beautiful. Thank you, dear. I haven't had a new thimble in ages. I didn't think anyone remembered my collection." She studied Katie's face, trying to understand her mood. "And how did you and David get along?"

"Just fine."

"Just fine? Is that all? You don't sound very excited."

"No, really, the day was great. We talked about everything. He's so wonderful, Gram. I just love him." Her face reddened with that admission, but Gram seemed not to notice, except for a slight smile that Katie didn't catch. She hurried on. "Did you know he was a double major in college? Agronomy and English? Can you believe that combination? English, just because he was interested in it. I *knew* he was an English major."

"Sounds fascinating," Gram responded with an over-the-glasses look. "But?"

"But what?"

"There's something troubling you. You're not telling your old grandmother everything."

Katie let out a huge sigh that ended in a laugh. "How do you know so much?"

"Oh, I just do. Now, come on, out with it."

"Well," Katie began hesitantly, "I don't know, it just seems sometimes he treats me kind of like I'm his sister."

"Uh-huh," Gram said, with a tone of skepticism. "And since when do brothers and sisters have big kissing scenes out in a cornfield?"

Katie laughed. "I knew I shouldn't have told you about that. Okay, since you must know, that day he really kissed me. I mean really kissed me. Now don't look so shocked. Remember, you're the one who asked. But I guess that was a once-in-a-lifetime thing. Now he's so . . . so . . . I don't know, cautious or something, like he's afraid he might be doing something he really shouldn't. Take tonight, for example, out on the porch. We spent the whole day together, and I thought we got along great, so he gives me a little peck like, well, like I was his sister. What's going on, anyway?"

Gram smiled a knowing smile. "Cold feet."

"Cold feet?"

"That's right. His feet are as cold as ice. You see, he did the commitment thing once, and it didn't work out so well. So now he's coming up with every excuse he can think of why he shouldn't try it again."

"Then why in the world did he ask me to go today if that's the way he feels?"

Gram smiled. "That's easy. He doesn't know *how* he feels. He's like that two-headed fella you were talking about."

Katie laughed. "You mean Dr. Jekyll and Mr. Hyde? He didn't have two heads. He just had two personalities."

"Well, whatever," Gram said. "That's the way David is. In his heart, he knows he's crazy about you, but then his head keeps getting in the way."

Katie had slipped off her shoes, and now she tucked her feet up next to her in the chair. "You may be on to something," she said thoughtfully. "He does almost seem like two people. Like the first time he kissed me, I was so sure it meant as much to him as it did to me. So what happens? He stays away like I have the plague."

"There, you see," Gram said triumphantly, "just like I said. You must have caught him with his guard down, but then afterward he started thinking too much." Gram's curiosity got the best of her. "What did you do that day to finally get him to kiss you?" She was suddenly embarrassed at her own question. "No, never mind. You don't have to answer that. I'm just a nosy old grandmother."

"No, it's no big deal." Katie laughed nervously. "Well, I guess that's not exactly true. It's just that I did something really stupid. Now, don't get mad when I tell you this, but the truth is I whacked him in the head with a dirt clod."

Gram's mouth gaped. "You what?"

Katie smiled remembering it all over again. "I knew you wouldn't like it. I threw a clod at him and accidentally hit him in the back of the head."

Gram still hadn't recovered. "You say accidentally?"

"Well, I did throw at him, but it was just dumb luck I hit him. At least in the head."

"And he kissed you because of that? You must have knocked the poor boy cuckoo."

"Well, it wasn't just because of that. One thing led to another, and before we knew it . . . well, you know." She flexed her arm. "Hey, maybe I should warm up the old arm and try again." They both laughed.

"No, dear, I think you're going to have to let him figure out his feelings without any more blows to the head."

"But do you think he ever will?"

"He will. He will. Give him time." She sounded confident, but inside she wasn't that sure, given David Cairn's track record.

Katie shook her head. "So how am I supposed to know when he figures it all out for himself?"

"You'll know," Gram said emphatically. "Don't worry, you'll know." She leaned back in her chair again and took up her stitching hoop. She was already wondering what more she could do to help things along.

Chapter Nineteen

The first field Katie had planted was tall enough to be cultivated. Weeds were already shouldering their way out of the ground in the middle of the corn rows, looking for their share of water and fertilizer, so they had to go. She headed out to the field with the cultivator mounted on the tractor, still another new experience for her. She found the job tedious, even more so than planting. She had to keep her eyes glued to the row marker to keep from plowing out the precious corn plants with the cultivator. She crept through the field at a slow speed all morning, covering little ground. She felt a little more comfortable in the afternoon, and upped her speed. Three or four times, though, the tractor drifted off-line and sheared off a swath of healthy corn plants six rows across before she could get the tractor going straight again.

Monotony was the problem. It made her so sleepy. Especially right after lunch. The rows of corn came at her in a never-ending flow until she was hypnotized. Her eyes glazed over for just a second, that's all it took, until she snapped back among the living to the sight of the tiny corn stalks toppling like miniature trees. She jerked the wheel and jammed her foot on the clutch. She sat looking out the back of the cab, frowning. The damage looked like a slash across the field. *If I keep this up, there won't be a darned thing left in the fall to harvest,* she thought.

Frustrating—that's what it was. Made the more so because she didn't have the luxury of daydreaming about David. The only time she could really think about him was at night, when she went to bed. And that didn't last long, as tired as she was. She would get some good thoughts going, only to wake with a start, the sun shining in her eyes through the space at the edge of her blinds. And as the week wore on, when she *did* think about him, she always ended with the same question. Where in the world was he anyway? Here it was already Wednesday, and she hadn't seen him or even heard from him since Saturday. Maybe she had read too much into last Saturday. If she hadn't, then he ought to be showing just a little more interest. If Gram was right in her assessment, his head must have won out entirely over his heart.

She dragged into the house at noon and washed up for lunch. She splashed water on her face and stared at herself in the mirror. A pair of bloodshot eyes looked back. She slipped into her chair.

"David stopped by this morning," Gram said brightly.

Katie looked up. "He did? Where in the world has he been?"

"He didn't say. I guess he's been busy just like you. He dropped off your bottle of wine and said to tell you hello."

Katie reached for a slice of bread. "That's big of him. His cold feet don't seem to be thawing any, do they?"

"Now, dear, don't be discouraged. Like I said, he's been busy. He and Otis have been moving cattle or something."

"Yeah, sure. But he wasn't too busy to stop to see you." She was in some kind of a mood.

Katie helped Gram with the dishes that evening and then dropped into a chair in the living room to read the newspaper. After only a few minutes, she tossed it aside. "I can't keep my mind on anything tonight. All I can see is corn coming at me." She stood and stretched. "I think I'll drive over to see Becky. Maybe she can get me out of the mood I'm in.''

Gram smiled up at her granddaughter. ''Good idea, dear. You've just been working too hard. That's what your problem is.'' She knew better when she said it.

''Sure, Gram.'' She headed for the door. ''I'll be back early.''

Katie sat in the living room waiting for Becky to pour coffee. She could hear the gravel voice of Otis from the nursery. He was doing his version of ''Inky Dinky Spider'' for Lena. The baby's giggles could mean only one thing— his performance wasn't bringing on sleep. Katie was looking about the room as Becky came in with the coffee. ''Did you keep your room this neat when you were a teenager?''

Becky smiled uncomfortably. ''Just about. I had to, or I'd catch it from my stepmother.''

Katie nodded. ''I'm sorry. I didn't mean to dig up bad memories. Hey, the bright side is, she made a housekeeper out of you.''

''That's about the only good thing you could say about her.'' She wanted to change the subject. ''Tell me about last Saturday. Where'd you go again? The Amana Colonies?''

''Oh, you'd love it there. The food! You've never tasted such food in your life.'' She tugged at her jeans. ''I gained five pounds.''

''Oh, I know that's not true. You look as thin as ever.'' Becky took a sip of her coffee. ''What did you two do there? Tell me everything.''

Katie described the day from start to finish with obvious relish. Becky watched her closely. When the story was done, Katie shrugged. ''I guess that's about it. Except I had a wonderful time.'' Her face clouded. ''I don't know about David though.''

"Why, what do you mean? Why wouldn't he have had a good time?"

"That's a good question. I thought he did. He said he did anyway. But I haven't heard from him since Saturday. Not one word. Wouldn't you think he'd at least call?"

Just then Otis tiptoed out of the nursery in his stocking feet and closed the door carefully behind him. "Hey, neighbor," he said, grinning at Katie. She tipped her coffee cup at him.

"She finally asleep?" Becky asked.

"Yep. I wore her down with my singin'."

"*That's* what that was," Katie said. "I thought one of your cows was sick."

Otis let out a roar and slammed a hand over his mouth as Becky shushed him, pointing at Lena's door. "Whoops." His voice became little more than a whisper. "You got a wide mean streak in ya, Katie Rourke. A mean streak I'm tellin' ya." His smile, and especially his eyes, made it obvious he didn't mean a word he was saying. He should have stopped while he was ahead, though. What he came out with next didn't set quite so well. "You been pickin' at my boss like that, ain't ya? He's been growlin' around like a bear with a sore paw all week long."

Katie's smile faded.

"Otis, mind your mouth," Becky ordered.

"What'd I put my foot in this time?" Otis said. "I didn't mean nothin' by it."

Thursday, Friday, Saturday—nothing. He didn't stop by once. He didn't even drive by, that she noticed. And he didn't call. If Gram was right, his head had gotten firm control of his heart. But she was afraid Otis might be on to something. She'd said or done something on the Amana trip to upset him. For the life of her, she couldn't figure out what. She replayed the whole day in her head to see what could have gone wrong. Nothing that she could remember.

"Why don't you call David and invite him for Sunday dinner?" Gram asked as they settled in the living room Saturday evening.

"So is that your latest plan of attack? I should take the initiative now?"

"Isn't that what women do in the nineties?"

Katie smiled. "Maybe you're right. Okay, I'll give it a try just for you, but I think it's a waste of time." She was gone less than three minutes before she dropped back into her chair.

"Well?" Gram asked.

"We don't need to worry about defrosting another chicken. He has other plans."

"What other plans?"

"I don't know. He didn't say."

Gram held a finished needlework project up for inspection. "What *did* he say?"

"Not much of anything. As far as I'm concerned, Mr. David Cairn can go take one big flying leap. I'm sick and tired of sitting around waiting for him to get over his failed marriage."

"Now, dear," Gram consoled, "don't be too hard on him." Inside, though, she had to admit to a big loss of confidence that the man would ever come around.

David jammed the phone onto its wall mount. He bounced his forehead lightly off the wall by the phone three times. "What is wrong with me?" he said out loud. "I sounded like some kind of idiot." He ran his fingers through his hair. *Did I tell her I'm taking Mom and Dad to Des Moines?* he thought. No, of course not. He picked up the phone. *I'll call her back.* He slammed it down again. *That will sound really stupid. I've tried staying away from her till I can get my head to stay on straight, but nothing works*. He sprawled back in an easy chair and stared dejectedly up at the ceiling.

Tuesday morning the sharp point on one of Katie's cultivator sweeps caught a rock and snapped off. She didn't notice the damage until she raised the cultivator at the end of the row. She put the tractor in high gear and headed to the house to see if she could handle the repair. She had a new sweep, but getting the old, broken one off was going to be another matter altogether. She struggled with it for half an hour with no luck. The old nut was rusted in place. She tried a shot of liquid wrench, put an extension on the socket handle, pounded on the thing with a hammer, but nothing worked. It was a sweltering, muggy day, a late afternoon storm was forecast. She wanted to finish the field before the rain came. She was hot, sweaty, and more than a little out of sorts. David's car pulled into the driveway.

She mopped her brow with the sleeve of her T-shirt and adjusted her U of I cap. He stepped out of the car and slammed the door. She watched him approach.

"Having trouble?" he asked.

"Now just what would give you that idea?" she growled.

He smiled. "The smoke coming out of your ears was a pretty good tip-off."

"Very funny." She turned her back on him and put the socket wrench on the nut. "Gram's in the house if you came to see her."

"Oh, well, I was . . . I was just wondering about you."

"I'm just fine. Don't I look like it? I was fine yesterday and the day before that and the day before that and the day . . ."

He interrupted her. "Here let me help you with that." He reached for the wrench.

She jerked it away from him. "I can do it myself, thank you."

He stood with his hands dangling awkwardly at his sides watching her as she adjusted the wrench again. ''I was just going to tell you . . .'' He hesitated, and she ignored him. ''Oh, never mind.'' He went slowly to his car, hoping to be called back. Katie heard each footstep on the crushed rock loud in her ears. She wanted to say something, but couldn't bring herself to do it. She gave the socket handle a mighty jerk out of frustration more than anything as the car door slammed, and the nut snapped free. As the Buick turned out of the lane, she dropped heavily on the ground by the tractor and buried her face in her hands. She cried like she hadn't cried since the day she found out her mom and dad had been killed.

The rain started late that afternoon. Katie had been watching the buildup of clouds since lunch, and she didn't like the looks of it. The green cast to the sky worried her most of all. She headed out of the field at the first large drops of rain, and by the time she reached the lane, she needed to click on the big windshield wipers. She ran the tractor into the machine shed and cut the engine. The rain was already drumming on the metal roof in a steady staccato. By the time she climbed down out of the tractor, the noise on the roof had become deafening. One glance out the overhead door told her why. Pea-size hail was beating hard against the ground.

She closed the overhead door and opened the smaller one to watch the storm. The wind had picked up, and the trees were bending under its force. The ground was already white with hail. She hoped Gram had seen her drive in, or she would be worried to death. She watched the hailstones tear leaves out of the maple standing in the front yard, and she felt a sickening feeling in her stomach when she thought about what was happening to her corn. The storm was over in ten minutes, at least the worst part. The rain came more gently for another twenty minutes or so, but she was able to run to the house. Gram was waiting by the door.

"Wasn't that awful?" she said. She was wringing her hands. "I was so glad when I saw you drive in just ahead of it. Why, the windows on your tractor would be broken out, wouldn't they? I thought the windows in the house were going to go."

"You should have heard it on the metal roof of the machine shed."

"Do you think it hurt your beautiful corn?"

"I'm afraid so, Gram. Just look at the trees. There are branches down all over. We'll check around when the rain stops."

The clouds rolled on past in another forty-five minutes, and the sun broke out again. But it was twenty degrees cooler outside. Katie and Gram took the pickup to the first field just south of the house. Katie could see before she got out of the truck how bad things were. The stalks of corn which had reached nearly to her knees just the night before were shredded and broken and beaten into the ground. The centers of the rows were still white with the hail. She made a twenty-yard circle, slogging in the mud. The damage was complete. She trudged back to the pickup. Gram could tell with one look at Katie's face that things weren't good.

"How bad is it?" she asked.

"It's a total loss, as far as I can see. It isn't just flattened, it's broken off. It doesn't look like any of it will come back. That's the end of it all."

"Oh, Katie, I'm so sorry." She laid a hand on her granddaughter's arm. "You worked so hard, and it was so beautiful."

"It really was, wasn't it?" She fought back the tears. "I was so proud." She dabbed at each eye with the sleeve of her T-shirt. "I know Dad was proud too." She started the truck, and the two drove on quietly to the rest of the fields. The corn was slashed and beaten beyond recovery in all of them. Next Katie headed south. The damage began to lessen one mile from her farm, and in two miles there was little hail showing in the fields and the corn looked wind-blown but nothing more. They drove north and found the same pattern.

"The worst of it can't be more than two or three miles wide," said Katie as she looked out the window. "We're smack in the middle of it." She had kept a brave face for the sake of her grandmother, but now she couldn't hold the tears back any longer. "I've lost everything, Gram. It's not fair. It's just not fair."

Chapter Twenty

It was just past ten-thirty the next morning when David tapped on the Rourke front door and stepped inside. "Anybody home?" he called.

Gram stuck her head around the corner from the kitchen. "Well, hello, stranger. Come in, come in." He stepped into the kitchen. Gram took one look at him and raised an eyebrow. She had never seen him so agitated.

"I'm sorry I wasn't here after the storm, but I was out of town—Des Moines. Dad just got out of the hospital this morning, and we came straight home."

She put a hand on his shoulder. "What happened? Is Frank all right? Why didn't you call?"

"Oh, he's fine. Nothing serious. He had cataract surgery yesterday. That's why I couldn't come to dinner Sunday. I took the folks down Sunday afternoon, and I should have told Katie that when she called." He continued breathlessly. "Anyway, Dad's surgery went fine, but they decided to keep him overnight. He was so dizzy he couldn't stand. He's feeling better today though." David was standing by the table with his hands resting on the back of a chair. He glanced into the living room. "Is Katie around? I heard about the hail when I stopped for gas in town. I just came from her fields. They're a mess. I thought she could use some cheering up." He hesitated. "I should have been here for her."

Gram's eyebrow raised ever so slightly at his last words.

181

She dug for a tissue in her apron pocket and dabbed at the corners of her eyes. "I'm afraid it's too late for that. Oh, David, I wish you could have been here too. Maybe you could have done something with her. I've never seen her like this. Things were going so well, and now . . ." Her voice trailed off. "I'm afraid this hail thing has got her down real bad. She says there's no way she can go on."

Gram stuck her hands in her apron pockets and hung her head in dejection. "She called her school back in Illinois to make sure she could still have her job." She shook her head. "I told her she didn't have to be in such a hurry to decide things, but you know how she is. Makes up her mind in a second and that's that. Oh, I'm sick about having to leave, but what's an old woman to do? I can't stay here by myself." Gram blew her nose loudly. "I've never known her to be so bitter. That's what worries me the most. She was going on and on, saying she hopes everybody's happy now she's lost everything. Now you know that just isn't like her—to feel sorry for herself like that. I got real upset with her. Told her nobody around here would wish bad luck on a neighbor." She dabbed at her eyes again. "If you'd been here, maybe you could have talked some sense into that head of hers, but it's probably all for the best. She ran out. You must have just missed her. She was on her way to see Stan Peters at the bank. She's decided to sell, and the faster the better. Maybe you can still catch her if you hurry."

He was at the door before the words were out of her mouth. "I hope I'm not too late," he shouted over his shoulder as the door slammed. Gram went to the window to watch him rush to his car.

He drove as fast as he dared on the mile of gravel, still sloppy from yesterday's rain, before he reached the hard-surface road that would take him to town. Once on the asphalt, he pushed the Buick well beyond the speed limit. His thoughts were a jumble. *What a total jerk I've been.*

Like staying away was going to solve anything. I had two perfect chances to tell her how I felt. So what do I do? Blow 'em both. Now it may be too late. I've got to tell her how I feel—if she'll even listen now. At least I can stop her from selling out for no reason. She doesn't need to do anything that desperate. It's not too late in the season to plant soybeans, if she's willing to start over. She would have known that if I'd been here to tell her.

He slowed as he reached the city limits, and headed straight to the town square, where he grabbed the first parking space he saw. He was on the corner opposite from the bank, and he sprinted through the square, skirting around the white-domed courthouse at its center. That's when he saw Katie. She was just getting out of her pickup by the bank. He cut across the lawn waving his arms. "Katie!" he shouted at the top of his lungs. A few shoppers on the sidewalk turned to see what the commotion was all about. "Wait up!" he called. Katie stopped in her tracks at the sound of her name.

She watched him as he crossed the street. His hair was standing on end, and he had a wild look about him. "What is wrong with you?" she asked as he came up to her, breathing hard from his sprint.

"We need to talk," he managed between gasps.

"What on earth about?" Now he was beginning to worry her. "Is something wrong? Is it Gram?"

"No, she's fine." He was looking about frantically. "Let's find someplace." He reached for her hand and led her across the street to a park bench in the town square. It was all a whirl for her. After the way she'd acted the other day, she didn't think he would ever speak to her again.

"Are you feeling all right?" she asked.

"I'm fine." He was finally beginning to calm down, now that he knew he was going to get to say what needed to be said. Even if he couldn't stop her, at least he'd have his say. "Just sit down and listen."

"Yes, sir," Katie said obediently.

He took a deep breath and started. "First off, I don't want you to leave."

"You what?"

"I know, I know," he blundered on. "I haven't been acting that way, but that's because I've been such a fool. Like last weekend. Our day together meant more than I wanted to admit. That's why I've been staying away from you. That makes a lot of sense, doesn't it. I guess I've been afraid of you." Her eyes showed a flicker of surprise. "No, I mean it. I've been afraid of getting too close. I kept remembering my botched-up marriage. I didn't want that to happen again. Ever. But what can I do? I can't keep you out of my head for ten minutes at a time. I hate to imagine my life without you in it." He took another deep breath. "Am I making any sense at all?"

Katie was staring at him with her mouth open. "Oh, yes, you're making perfect sense." Thanks to Gram, she thought to herself.

The way she said it as much as what she said gave him his first real hope. His eyebrows arched in surprise. She was still here listening. Maybe there *was* still a chance. He reached over and took her hand. "Katie, I think I love you." He shook his head. "No, no, let me say that all over again. I *know* I love you."

"Well, it's about time," she said with a smile starting, "because I know I love you, David Cairn. I have for a long time."

Her words were more than he could have ever hoped for. He reached for her then and pulled her toward him. He found her lips and crushed them with his own. It was like a certain earlier kiss, only this time without the mud. If he had opened with that kiss only moments earlier, he could have saved a lot of words.

Katie moved her hand from the back of his neck and touched his shoulder gently to draw them apart. "Wow, that's more like it,'' she said breathlessly, ''but look where we are. We're going to draw a crowd. We've got to find a more private place for our kissing scenes.''

''I couldn't agree more,'' he said as he watched her eyes with a certain gleam in his own. Suddenly he sat back. Wait, there's something else. I almost forgot.'' She watched him expectantly. ''I checked your hail damage.'' He shook his head. ''It's pretty bad.''

''Tell me something I don't know.''

''But that's not all.'' He took her hand. ''You don't have to leave. It's not too late to replant. But it'll have to be soybeans, and the right variety.''

''I know,'' she said, smiling.

''It'll be hard work, but Otis and I can help out,'' he went on, as if he hadn't heard her. Suddenly he stopped. ''What do you mean you know?''

''I just picked up my seed beans at the elevator. They're in the back of the pickup.''

''You mean you're not quitting to go back to Illinois?''

''Heavens no. Whatever gave you that idea? Haven't you learned anything about me? I don't give up that easily.''

''But weren't you heading for the bank to tell Stan Peters to put your land up for sale?''

''No, silly, I was on my way to Daly Pharmacy to get a prescription for Gram.''

The truth suddenly dawned on him. He smiled and nodded his head slowly. ''Don't ever play poker with that grandmother of yours.''

''What do you mean?'' Suddenly she let out a quick breath that ended in a laugh. ''No, you don't mean it. Gram told you all those things?''

''She sure did. Is it true you called your school this morning about teaching next fall?''

''Of course not. My former principal called *me* and asked if I was coming back. I told him no. Did she tell you that too?''

"She sure did. That little conniver." He was remembering especially her skill with the tissue.

"Let me ask you one thing. Did she have her fingers crossed?"

He laughed. "How should I know? Why?"

"Because she thinks it's not a lie if you have your fingers crossed."

He slipped his arm around her and pulled her close again. "Well, I'll forgive her this one time. After all, if it hadn't been for what she told me, I might not be sitting here with you."

"I know," Katie said as she turned toward him. "She just wanted to knock some sense into that head of yours. She thought that was a better idea than a whack with a dirt clod." Just before their lips met, she saw the glimmer of understanding in his eyes.